William Wordsworth

Lyrical Ballads, with a few Other Poems (1800)

Volume I

William Wordsworth

Lyrical Ballads, with a few Other Poems (1800)

Volume I

1st Edition | ISBN: 978-3-73266-490-0

Place of Publication: Frankfurt am Main, Germany

Year of Publication: 2018

Outlook Verlag GmbH, Deutschland.

Reproduction of the original.

LYRICAL BALLADS,

WITH OTHER POEMS.

IN TWO VOLUMES.

1800

By W. WORDSWORTH.

Quam nihil ad genium, Papiniane, tuum!

VOL. I.

SECOND EDITION.

CONTENTS.

PREFACE.

The First Volume of these Poems has already been submitted to general perusal. It was published, as an experiment which, I hoped, might be of some use to ascertain, how far, by fitting to metrical arrangement a selection of the real language of men in a state of vivid sensation, that sort of pleasure and that quantity of pleasure may be imparted, which a Poet may rationally endeavour to impart.

I had formed no very inaccurate estimate of the probable effect of those Poems: I flattered myself that they who should be pleased with them would read them with more than common pleasure: and on the other hand I was well aware that by those who should dislike them they would be read with more than common dislike. The result has differed from my expectation in this only, that I have pleased a greater number, than I ventured to hope I should please.

For the sake of variety and from a consciousness of my own weakness I was induced to request the assistance of a Friend, who furnished me with the Poems of the ANCIENT MARINER, the FOSTER-MOTHER'S TALE, the NIGHTINGALE, the DUNGEON, and the Poem entitled LOVE. I should not, however, have requested this assistance, had I not believed that the poems of my Friend would in a great measure have the same tendency as my own, and that, though there would be found a difference, there would be found no discordance in the colours of our style; as our opinions on the subject of poetry do almost entirely coincide.

Several of my Friends are anxious for the success of these Poems from a belief, that if the views, with which they were composed, were indeed realized, a class of Poetry would be produced, well adapted to interest mankind permanently, and not unimportant in the multiplicity and in the quality of its moral relations: and on this account they have advised me to prefix a systematic defence of the theory, upon which the poems were written. But I was unwilling to undertake the task, because I knew that on this occasion the Reader would look coldly upon my arguments, since I might be suspected of having been principally influenced by the selfish and foolish hope of *reasoning* him into an approbation of these particular Poems: and I was still more unwilling to undertake the task, because adequately to display my opinions and fully to enforce my arguments would require a space wholly disproportionate to the nature of a preface. For to treat the subject with the clearness and coherence, of which I believe it susceptible, it would be necessary to give a full account of the present state of the public taste in this country, and to determine how far this taste is healthy or depraved; which again could not be determined, without pointing out, in what manner language and the human mind act and react on each other, and without retracing the revolutions not of literature alone but likewise of society itself. I have therefore altogether declined to enter regularly upon this defence; yet I am sensible, that there would be some impropriety in abruptly obtruding upon the Public, without a few words of introduction, Poems so materially different from those, upon which general approbation is at present bestowed.

It is supposed, that by the act of writing in verse an Author makes a formal engagement that he will gratify certain known habits of association, that he not only thus apprizes the Reader that certain classes of ideas and expressions will be found in his book, but that others will be carefully excluded. This exponent or symbol held forth by metrical language must in different aeras of literature have excited very different expectations: for example, in the age of Catullus Terence and Lucretius, and that of Statius or Claudian, and in our own country, in the age of Shakespeare and Beaumont and Fletcher, and that of Donne and Cowley, or Dryden, or Pope. I will not take upon me to determine the exact import of the promise which by the act of writing in verse an Author in the present day makes to his Reader; but I am certain it will appear to many persons that I have not fulfilled the terms of an engagement thus voluntarily contracted. I hope therefore the Reader will not censure me, if I attempt to state what I have proposed to myself to perform, and also, (as far as the limits of a preface will permit) to explain some of the chief reasons which have determined me in the choice of my purpose: that at least he may be spared any unpleasant feeling of disappointment, and that I myself may be protected from the most dishonorable accusation which can be brought against an Author, namely, that of an indolence which prevents him from endeavouring to ascertain what is his duty, or, when his duty is ascertained prevents him from performing it.

The principal object then which I proposed to myself in these Poems was to make the incidents of common life interesting by tracing in them, truly though not ostentatiously, the primary laws of our nature: chiefly as far as regards the manner in which we associate ideas in a state of excitement. Low and rustic life was generally chosen because in that situation the essential passions of the heart find a better soil in which they can attain their maturity, are less under restraint, and speak a plainer and more emphatic language; because in that situation our elementary feelings exist in a state of greater simplicity and consequently may be more accurately contemplated and more forcibly communicated; because the manners of rural life germinate from those elementary feelings; and from the necessary character of rural occupations are more easily comprehended; and are more durable; and lastly, because in that situation the passions of men are incorporated with the beautiful and permanent forms of nature. The language too of these men is adopted (purified indeed from what appear to be its real defects, from all lasting and rational causes of dislike or disgust) because such men hourly communicate with the best objects from which the best part of language is originally derived; and because, from their rank in society and the sameness and narrow circle of their intercourse, being less under the action of social vanity they convey their feelings and notions in simple and unelaborated expressions. Accordingly such a language arising out of repeated experience and regular feelings is a more permanent and a far more philosophical language than that which is frequently substituted for it by Poets, who think that they are conferring honour upon themselves and their art in proportion as they separate themselves from the sympathies of men, and indulge in arbitrary and capricious habits of expression in order to furnish food for fickle tastes and fickle appetites of their own creation.[1]

[Footnote 1: It is worth while here to observe that the affecting parts of Chaucer are almost always expressed in language pure and universally intelligible even to this day.]

I cannot be insensible of the present outcry against the triviality and meanness both of thought and language, which some of my contemporaries have occasionally introduced into their metrical compositions; and I acknowledge that this defect where it exists, is more dishonorable to the Writer's own character than false refinement or arbitrary innovation, though I should contend at the same time that it is far less pernicious in the sum of its consequences. From such verses the Poems in these volumes will be found distinguished at least by one mark of difference, that each of them has a worthy *purpose*. Not that I mean to say, that I always began to write with a distinct purpose formally conceived; but I believe that my habits of meditation have so formed my feelings, as that my descriptions of such objects as strongly excite those feelings, will be found to carry along with them a *purpose*. If in this opinion I am mistaken I can have little right to the name of a Poet. For all good poetry is the spontaneous overflow of powerful feelings; but though this be true, Poems to which any value can be attached, were never produced on any variety of subjects but by a man who being possessed of more than usual organic sensibility had also thought long and deeply. For our continued influxes of feeling are modified and directed by our thoughts, which are indeed the representatives of all our past feelings; and as by contemplating the relation of these general representatives to each other, we discover what is really important to men, so by the repetition and continuance of this act feelings connected with important subjects will be nourished, till at length, if we be originally possessed of much organic sensibility, such habits of mind will be produced that by obeying blindly and mechanically the impulses of those habits we shall describe objects and utter sentiments of such a nature and in such connection with each other, that the understanding of the being to whom we address ourselves, if he be in a healthful state of association, must necessarily be in some degree enlightened, his taste exalted, and his affections ameliorated.

I have said that each of these poems has a purpose. I have also informed my Reader what this purpose will be found principally to be: namely to illustrate the manner in which our feelings and ideas are associated in a state of excitement. But speaking in less general language, it is to follow the fluxes and refluxes of the mind when agitated by the great and simple affections of our nature. This object I have endeavoured in these short essays to attain by various means; by tracing the maternal passion through many of its more subtle windings, as in the poems of the IDIOT BOY and the MAD MOTHER; by accompanying the last struggles of a human being at the approach of death, cleaving in solitude to life and society, as in the Poem of the FORSAKEN INDIAN; by shewing, as in the Stanzas entitled WE ARE SEVEN, the perplexity and obscurity which in childhood attend our notion of death, or rather our utter inability to admit that notion; or by displaying the strength of fraternal, or to speak more philosophically, of moral attachment when early associated with the great and beautiful objects of nature, as in THE BROTHERS; or, as in the Incident of SIMON LEE, by placing my Reader in the way of receiving from ordinary moral sensations another and more salutary impression than we are accustomed to receive from them. It has also been part of my general purpose to attempt to sketch characters under the influence of less impassioned feelings, as in the OLD MAN TRAVELLING, THE TWO THIEVES, &c. characters of which the elements are simple, belonging rather to nature than to manners, such as exist now and will probably always exist, and which from their constitution may be distinctly and profitably contemplated. I will not abuse the indulgence of my Reader by dwelling longer upon this subject; but it is proper that I should mention one other circumstance which distinguishes these Poems from the popular Poetry of the day; it is this, that the feeling therein developed gives importance to the action and situation and not the action and situation to the feeling. My meaning will be rendered perfectly intelligible by referring my Reader to the Poems entitled POOR SUSAN and the CHILDLESS FATHER, particularly to the last Stanza of the latter Poem.

I will not suffer a sense of false modesty to prevent me from asserting, that I point my Reader's attention to this mark of distinction far less for the sake of these particular Poems than from the general importance of the subject. The subject is indeed important! For the human mind is capable of excitement without the application of gross and violent stimulants; and he must have a very faint perception of its beauty and dignity who does not know this, and who does not further know that one being is elevated above another in proportion as he possesses this capability. It has therefore appeared to me that to endeavour to produce or enlarge this capability is one of the best services in which, at any period, a Writer can be engaged; but this service, excellent at all times, is especially so at the present day. For a multitude of causes unknown to former times are now acting with a combined force to blunt the discriminating powers of the mind, and unfitting it for all voluntary exertion to reduce it to a state of almost savage torpor. The most effective of these causes are the great national events which are daily taking place, and the encreasing accumulation of men in cities, where the uniformity of their occupations produces a craving for extraordinary incident which the rapid communication of intelligence hourly gratifies. To this tendency of life and manners the literature and theatrical exhibitions of the country have conformed themselves. The invaluable works of our elder writers, I had almost said the works of Shakespeare and Milton, are driven into neglect by frantic novels, sickly and stupid German Tragedies, and deluges of idle and extravagant stories in verse.—When I think upon this degrading thirst after outrageous stimulation I am almost ashamed to have spoken of the feeble effort with which I have endeavoured to counteract it; and reflecting upon the magnitude of the general evil, I should be oppressed with no dishonorable melancholy, had I not a deep impression of certain inherent and indestructible qualities of the human mind, and likewise of certain powers in the great and permanent objects that act upon it which are equally inherent and indestructible; and did I not further add to this impression a belief that the time is approaching when the evil will be systematically opposed by men of greater powers and with far more distinguished success.

Having dwelt thus long on the subjects and aim of these Poems, I shall request the Reader's permission to apprize him of a few circumstances relating to their *style*, in order, among other reasons, that I may not be censured for not having performed what I never attempted. Except in a very few instances the Reader will find no personifications of abstract ideas in these volumes, not that I mean to censure such personifications: they may be well fitted for certain sorts of composition, but in these Poems I propose to myself to imitate, and, as far as possible, to adopt the very language of men, and I do not find that such personifications make any regular or natural part of that language. I wish to keep my Reader in the company of flesh and blood, persuaded that by so doing I shall interest him. Not but that I believe that others who pursue a different track may interest him likewise: I do not interfere with their claim, I only wish to prefer a different claim of my own. There will also be found in these volumes little of what is usually called poetic diction; I have taken as much pains to avoid it as others ordinarily take to produce it; this I have done for the reason already alleged, to bring my language near to the language of men, and further, because the pleasure which I have proposed to myself to impart is of a kind very different from that which is supposed by many persons to be the proper object of poetry. I do not know how without being culpably particular I can give my Reader a more exact notion of the style in which I wished these poems to be written than by informing him that I have at all times endeavoured to look steadily at my subject, consequently I hope it will be found that there is in these Poems little falsehood of description, and that my ideas are expressed in language fitted to their respective importance. Something I must have gained by this practice, as it is friendly to one property of all good poetry, namely good sense; but it has necessarily cut me off from a large portion of phrases and figures of speech which from father to son have long been regarded as the common inheritance of Poets. I have also thought it expedient to restrict myself still further, having abstained from the use of many expressions, in themselves proper and beautiful, but which have been foolishly repeated by bad Poets till such feelings of disgust are connected with them as it is scarcely possible by any art of association to overpower.

If in a Poem there should be found a series of lines, or even a single line, in which the language, though naturally arranged and according to the strict laws of metre, does not differ from that of prose, there is a numerous class of critics who, when they stumble upon these prosaisms as they call them, imagine that they have made a notable discovery, and exult over the Poet as over a man ignorant of his own profession. Now these men would establish a canon of criticism which the Reader will conclude he must utterly reject if he wishes to be pleased with these volumes. And it would be a most easy task to prove to him that not only the language of a large portion of every good poem, even of the most elevated character, must necessarily, except with reference to the metre, in no respect differ from that of good prose, but likewise that some of the most interesting parts of the best poems will be found to be strictly the language of prose when prose is well written. The truth of this assertion might be demonstrated by innumerable passages from almost all the poetical writings, even of Milton himself. I have not space for much quotation; but, to illustrate the subject in a general manner, I will here adduce a short composition of Gray, who was at the head of those who by their reasonings have attempted to widen the space of separation betwixt Prose and Metrical composition, and was more than any other man curiously elaborate in the structure of his own poetic diction.

In vain to me the smiling mornings shine,
And reddening Phoebus lifts his golden fire:
The birds in vain their amorous descant join,
Or chearful fields resume their green attire:

These ears alas! for other notes repine;
A different object do these eyes require;
My lonely anguish melts no heart but mine;
And in my breast the imperfect joys expire; Yet
Morning smiles the busy race to cheer, And
new-born pleasure brings to happier men; The
fields to all their wonted tribute bear;
To warm their little loves the birds complain.
I fruitless mourn to him that cannot hear
And weep the more because I weep in vain.

It will easily be perceived that the only part of this Sonnet which is of any value is the lines printed in Italics: it is equally obvious that except in the rhyme, and in the use of the single word "fruitless" for fruitlessly, which is so far a defect, the language of these lines does in no respect differ from that of prose.

Is there then, it will be asked, no essential difference between the language of prose and metrical composition? I answer that there neither is nor can be any essential difference. We are fond of tracing the resemblance between Poetry and Painting, and, accordingly, we call them Sisters: but where shall we find bonds of connection sufficiently strict to typify the affinity betwixt metrical and prose composition? They both speak by and to the same organs; the bodies in which both of them are clothed may be said to be of the same substance, their affections are kindred and almost identical, not necessarily differing even in degree; Poetry [2] sheds no tears "such as Angels weep," but natural and human tears; she can boast of no celestial Ichor that distinguishes her vital juices from those of prose; the same human blood circulates through the veins of them both.

[Footnote 2: I here use the word "Poetry" (though against my own judgment) as opposed to the word Prose, and synonomous with metrical composition. But much confusion has been introduced into criticism by this contradistinction of Poetry and Prose, instead of the more philosophical one of Poetry and Science. The only strict antithesis to Prose is Metre.]

If it be affirmed that rhyme and metrical arrangement of themselves constitute a distinction which overturns what I have been saying on the strict affinity of metrical language with that of prose, and paves the way for other distinctions which the mind voluntarily admits, I answer that the distinction of rhyme and metre is regular and uniform, and not, like that which is produced by what is usually called poetic diction, arbitrary and subject to infinite caprices upon which no calculation whatever can be made. In the one case the Reader is utterly at the mercy of the Poet respecting what imagery or diction he may choose to connect with the passion, whereas in the other the metre obeys certain laws, to which the Poet and Reader both willingly submit because they are certain, and because no interference is made by them with the passion but such as the concurring testimony of ages has shewn to heighten and improve the pleasure which co-exists with it. It will now be proper to answer an obvious question, namely, why, professing these opinions have I written in verse? To this in the first place I reply, because, however I may have restricted myself, there is still left open to me what confessedly constitutes the most valuable object of all writing whether in prose or verse, the great and universal passions of men, the most general and interesting of their occupations, and the entire world of nature, from which I am at liberty to supply myself with endless combinations of forms and imagery. Now, granting for a moment that whatever is interesting in these objects may be as vividly described in prose, why am I to be condemned if to such description I have endeavoured to superadd the charm which by the consent of all nations is acknowledged to exist in metrical language? To this it will be answered, that a very small part of the pleasure given by Poetry depends upon the metre, and that it is injudicious to write in metre unless it be accompanied with the other artificial distinctions of style with which metre is usually accompanied, and that by such deviation more will be lost from the shock which will be thereby given to the Reader's associations than will be counterbalanced by any pleasure which he can derive from the general power of numbers. In answer to those who thus contend for the necessity of accompanying metre with certain appropriate colours of style in order to the accomplishment of its appropriate end, and who also, in my opinion, greatly under-rate the power of metre in itself, it might perhaps be almost sufficient to observe that poems are extant, written upon more humble subjects, and in a more naked and simple style than what I have aimed at, which poems have continued to give pleasure from generation to generation. Now, if nakedness and simplicity be a defect, the fact here mentioned affords a strong presumption that poems somewhat less naked and simple are capable of affording pleasure at the present day; and all that I am now attempting is to justify myself for having written under the impression of this belief.

But I might point out various causes why, when the style is manly, and the subject of some importance, words metrically arranged will long continue to impart such a pleasure to mankind as he who is sensible of the extent of that pleasure will be desirous to impart. The end of Poetry is to produce excitement in coexistence with an overbalance of pleasure. Now, by the supposition, excitement is an unusual and irregular state of the mind; ideas and feelings do not in that state succeed each other in accustomed order. But if the words by which this excitement is produced are in themselves powerful, or the images and feelings have an undue proportion of pain connected with them, there is some danger that the excitement may be carried beyond its proper bounds. Now the co-presence of something regular, something to which the mind has been accustomed when in an unexcited or a less excited state, cannot but have great efficacy in tempering and restraining the passion by an intertexture of ordinary feeling. This may be illustrated by appealing to the Reader's own experience of the reluctance with which he comes to the re-perusal of the distressful parts of Clarissa Harlowe, or the Gamester. While Shakespeare's writings, in the most pathetic scenes, never act upon us as pathetic beyond the bounds of pleasure—an effect which is in a great degree to be ascribed to small, but continual and regular impulses of pleasurable surprise from the metrical arrangement.—On the other hand (what it must be allowed will much more frequently happen) if the Poet's words should be incommensurate with the passion, and inadequate to raise the Reader to a height of desirable excitement, then, (unless the Poet's choice of his metre has been grossly injudicious) in the feelings of pleasure which the Reader has been accustomed to connect with metre in general, and in the feeling, whether chearful or melancholy, which he has been accustomed to connect with that particular movement of metre, there will be found something which will greatly contribute to impart passion to the words, and to effect the complex end which the Poet proposes to himself.

If I had undertaken a systematic defence of the theory upon which these poems are written, it would have been my duty to develope the various causes upon which the pleasure received from metrical language depends. Among the chief of these causes is to be reckoned a principle which must be well known to those who have made any of the Arts the object of accurate reflection; I mean the pleasure which the mind derives from the perception of similitude in dissimilitude. This principle is the great spring of the activity of our minds and their chief feeder. From this principle the direction of the sexual appetite, and all the passions connected with it take their origin: It is the life of our ordinary conversation; and upon the accuracy with which similitude in dissimilitude, and dissimilitude in similitude are perceived, depend our taste and our moral feelings. It would not have been a useless employment to have applied this principle to the consideration of metre, and to have shewn that metre is hence enabled to afford much pleasure, and to have pointed out in what manner that pleasure is produced. But my limits will not permit me to enter upon this subject, and I must content myself with a general summary.

I have said that Poetry is the spontaneous overflow of powerful feelings: it takes its origin from emotion recollected in tranquillity: the emotion is contemplated till by a species of reaction the tranquillity gradually disappears, and an emotion, similar to that which was before the subject of contemplation, is gradually produced, and does itself actually exist in the mind. In this mood successful composition generally begins, and in a mood similar to this it is carried on; but the emotion, of whatever kind and in whatever degree, from various causes is qualified by various pleasures, so that in describing any passions whatsoever, which are voluntarily described, the mind will upon the whole be in a state of enjoyment. Now if Nature be thus cautious in preserving in a state of enjoyment a being thus employed, the Poet ought to profit by the lesson thus held forth to him, and ought especially to take care, that whatever passions he communicates to his Reader, those passions, if his Reader's mind be sound and vigorous, should always be accompanied with an overbalance of pleasure. Now the music of harmonious metrical language, the sense of difficulty overcome, and the blind association of pleasure which has been previously received from works of rhyme or metre of the same or similar construction, all these imperceptibly make up a complex feeling of delight, which is of the most important use in tempering the painful feeling which will always be found intermingled with powerful descriptions of the deeper passions. This effect is always produced in pathetic and impassioned poetry; while in lighter compositions the ease and gracefulness with which the Poet manages his numbers are themselves confessedly a principal source of the gratification of the Reader. I might perhaps include all which it is *necessary* to say upon this subject by affirming what few persons will deny, that of two descriptions either of passions, manners, or characters, each of them equally well executed, the one in prose and the other in verse, the verse will be read a hundred times where the prose is read once. We see that Pope by the power of verse alone, has contrived to render the plainest common sense interesting, and even frequently to invest it with the appearance of passion. In consequence of these convictions I related in metre the Tale of GOODY BLAKE and HARRY GILL, which is one of the rudest of this collection. I wished to draw attention to the truth that the power of the human imagination is sufficient to produce such changes even in our physical nature as might almost appear miraculous. The truth is an important one; the fact (for it is a *fact*) is a valuable illustration of it. And I have the satisfaction of knowing that it has been communicated to many hundreds of people who would never have heard of it, had it not been narrated as a Ballad, and in a more impressive metre than is usual in Ballads.

Having thus adverted to a few of the reasons why I have written in verse, and why I have chosen subjects from common life, and endeavoured to bring my language near to the real language of men, if I have been too minute in pleading my own cause, I have at the same time been treating a subject of general interest; and it is for this reason that I request the Reader's permission to add a few words with reference solely to these particular poems, and to some defects which will probably be found in them. I am sensible that my associations must have sometimes been particular instead of general, and that, consequently, giving to things a false importance, sometimes from diseased impulses I may have written upon unworthy subject; but I am less apprehensive on this account, than that my language may frequently have suffered from those arbitrary connections of feelings and ideas with particular words, from which no man can altogether protect himself. Hence I have no doubt that in some instances feelings even of the ludicrous may be given to my Readers by expressions which appeared to me tender and pathetic. Such faulty expressions, were I convinced they were faulty at present, and that they must necessarily continue to be so, I would willingly take all reasonable pains to correct. But it is dangerous to make these alterations on the simple authority of a few individuals, or even of certain classes of men; for where the understanding of an Author is not convinced, or his feelings altered, this cannot be done without great injury to himself: for his own feelings are his stay and support, and if he sets them aside in one instance, he may be induced to repeat this act till his mind loses all confidence in itself and becomes utterly debilitated. To this it may be added, that the Reader ought never to forget that he is himself exposed to the same errors as the Poet, and perhaps in a much greater degree: for there can be no presumption in saying that it is not probable he will be so well acquainted with the various stages of meaning through which words have passed, or with the fickleness or stability of the relations of particular ideas to each other; and above all, since he is so much less interested in the subject, he may decide lightly and carelessly.

Long as I have detained my Reader, I hope he will permit me to caution him against a mode of false criticism which has been applied to Poetry in which the language closely resembles that of life and nature. Such verses have been triumphed over in parodies of which Dr. Johnson's Stanza is a fair specimen.

"I put my hat upon my head,
And walk'd into the Strand,
And there I met another man
Whose hat was in his hand."

Immediately under these lines I will place one of the most justly admired stanzas of the "*Babes* in the Wood."

"These pretty Babes with hand in hand
Went wandering up and down;
But never more they saw the Man
Approaching from the Town."

In both of these stanzas the words, and the order of the words, in no respect differ from the most unimpassioned conversation. There are words in both, for example, "the Strand," and "the Town," connected with none but the most familiar ideas; yet the one stanza we admit as admirable, and the other as a fair example of the superlatively contemptible. Whence arises this difference? Not from the metre, not from the language, not from the order of the words; but the *matter* expressed in Dr. Johnson's stanza is contemptible. The proper method of treating trivial and simple verses to which Dr. Johnson's stanza would be a fair parallelism is not to say this is a bad kind of poetry, or this is not poetry, but this wants sense; it is neither interesting in itself, nor can *lead* to any thing interesting; the images neither originate in that sane state of feeling which arises out of thought, nor can excite thought or feeling in the Reader. This is the only sensible manner of dealing with such verses: Why trouble yourself about the species till you have previously decided upon the genus? Why take pains to prove that an Ape is not a Newton when it is self-evident that he is not a man.

I have one request to make of my Reader, which is, that in judging these Poems he would decide by his own feelings genuinely, and not by reflection upon what will probably be the judgment of others. How common is it to hear a person say, "I myself do not object to this style of composition or this or that expression, but to such and such classes of people it will appear mean or ludicrous." This mode of criticism so destructive of all sound unadulterated judgment is almost universal: I have therefore to request that the Reader would abide independently by his own feelings, and that if he finds himself affected he would not suffer such conjectures to interfere with his pleasure.

If an Author by any single composition has impressed us with respect for his talents, it is useful to consider this as affording a presumption, that, on other occasions where we have been displeased, he nevertheless may not have written ill or absurdly; and, further, to give him so much credit for this one composition as may induce us to review what has displeased us with more care than we should otherwise have bestowed upon it. This is not only an act of justice, but in our decisions upon poetry especially, may conduce in a high degree to the improvement of our own taste: for an *accurate* taste in Poetry and in all the other arts, as Sir Joshua Reynolds has observed, is an *acquired* talent, which can only be produced by thought and a long continued intercourse with the best models of composition. This is mentioned not with so ridiculous a purpose as to prevent the most inexperienced Reader from judging for himself, (I have already said that I wish him to judge for himself;) but merely to temper the rashness of decision, and to suggest that if Poetry be a subject on which much time has not been bestowed, the judgment may be erroneous, and that in many cases it necessarily will be so.

I know that nothing would have so effectually contributed to further the end which I have in view as to have shewn of what kind the pleasure is, and how the pleasure is produced which is confessedly produced by metrical composition essentially different from what I have here endeavoured to recommend; for the Reader will say that he has been pleased by such composition and what can I do more for him? The power of any art is limited and he will suspect that if I propose to furnish him with new friends it is only upon condition of his abandoning his old friends. Besides, as I have said, the Reader is himself conscious of the pleasure which he has received from such composition, composition to which he has peculiarly attached the endearing name of Poetry; and all men feel an habitual gratitude, and something of an honorable bigotry for the objects which have long continued to please them: we not only wish to be pleased, but to be pleased in that particular way in which we have been accustomed to be pleased. There is a host of arguments in these feelings; and I should be the less able to combat them successfully, as I am willing to allow, that, in order entirely to enjoy the Poetry which I am recommending, it would be necessary to give up much of what is ordinarily enjoyed. But would my limits have permitted me to point out how this pleasure is produced, I might have removed many obstacles, and assisted my Reader in perceiving that the powers of language are not so limited as he may suppose; and that it is possible that poetry may give other enjoyments, of a purer, more lasting, and more exquisite nature. But this part of my subject I have been obliged altogether to omit: as it has been less my present aim to prove that the interest excited by some other kinds of poetry is less vivid, and less worthy of the nobler powers of the mind, than to offer reasons for presuming, that, if the object which I have proposed to myself were adequately attained, a species of poetry would be produced, which is genuine poetry; in its nature well adapted to interest mankind permanently, and likewise important in the multiplicity and quality of its moral relations. From what has been said, and from a perusal of the Poems, the Reader will be able clearly to perceive the object which I have proposed to myself: he will determine how far I have attained this object; and, what is a much more important question, whether it be worth attaining; and upon the decision of these two questions will rest my claim to the approbation of the public.

EXPOSTULATION AND REPLY.

"Why, William, on that old grey stone,
Thus for the length of half a day,
Why, William, sit you thus alone,
And dream your time away?"

"Where are your books? that light bequeath'd
To beings else forlorn and blind!
Up! Up! and drink the spirit breath'd
From dead men to their kind."

"You look round on your mother earth,
As if she for no purpose bore you;
As if you were her first-born birth,
And none had lived before you!"

One morning thus, by Esthwaite lake,
When life was sweet, I knew not why,
To me my good friend Matthew spake,
And thus I made reply.

"The eye it cannot chuse but see,
We cannot bid the ear be still;
Our bodies feel, where'er they be,
Against, or with our will."

"Nor less I deem that there are powers
Which of themselves our minds impress,
That we can feed this mind of ours
In a wise passiveness."

"Think you, mid all this mighty sum
Of things for ever speaking,
That nothing of itself will come,
But we must still be seeking?"

"—Then ask not wherefore, here, alone,
Conversing as I may,
I sit upon this old grey stone,
And dream my time away."

THE TABLES TURNED;

An Evening Scene, on the same Subject,

  Up! up! my friend, and clear your looks,
Why all this toil and trouble?
Up! up! my friend, and quit your books,
Or surely you'll grow double.

  The sun, above the mountain's head,
A freshening lustre mellow
Through all the long green fields has spread,
His first sweet evening yellow.

  Books! 'tis dull and endless strife,
Come, here the woodland linnet,
How sweet his music; on my life
There's more of wisdom in it.

  And hark! how blithe the throstle sings!
And he is no mean preacher;
Come forth into the light of things,
Let Nature be your teacher.

  She has a world of ready wealth,
Our minds and hearts to bless—
Spontaneous wisdom breathed by health,
Truth breathed by chearfulness.

  One impulse from a vernal wood
May teach you more of man;
Of moral evil and of good,
Than all the sages can.

  Sweet is the lore which nature brings;
Our meddling intellect
Mishapes the beauteous forms of things;
—We murder to dissect.

  Enough of science and of art;
Close up these barren leaves;
Come forth, and bring with you a heart
That watches and receives.

ANIMAL TRANQUILLITY & DECAY

A SKETCH.

  The little hedge-row birds
That peck along the road, regard him not.
He travels on, and in his face, his step,
His gait, is one expression; every limb,
His look and bending figure, all bespeak
A man who does not move with pain, but moves
With thought—He is insensibly subdued
To settled quiet: he is one by whom
All effort seems forgotten, one to whom
Long patience has such mild composure given,
That patience now doth seem a thing, of which
He hath no need. He is by nature led
To peace so perfect, that the young behold
With envy, what the old man hardly feels.
—I asked him whither he was bound, and what
The object of his journey; he replied
That he was going many miles to take
A last leave of his son, a mariner,
Who from a sea-fight had been brought to Falmouth,
And there was lying in an hospital.

THE COMPLAINT OF A FORSAKEN INDIAN WOMAN.

[*When a Northern Indian, from sickness, is unable to continue his journey with his companions; he is left behind, covered over with Deer-skins, and is supplied with water, food, and fuel if the situation of the place will afford it. He is informed of the track which his companions intend to pursue, and if he is unable to follow, or overtake them, he perishes alone in the Desart; unless he should have the good fortune to fall in with some other Tribes of Indians. It is unnecessary to add that the females are equally, or still more, exposed to the same fate. See that very interesting work,* Hearne's Journey *from* Hudson's Bay *to the* Northern Ocean. *In the high Northern Latititudes, as the same writer informs us, when the Northern Lights vary their position in the air, they make a rustling and a crackling noise. This circumstance is alluded to in the first stanza of the following poem.*]

THE COMPLAINT, etc.

Before I see another day,
Oh let my body die away!
In sleep I heard the northern gleams;
The stars they were among my dreams;
In sleep did I behold the skies,
I saw the crackling flashes drive;
And yet they are upon my eyes,
And yet I am alive.
Before I see another day,
Oh let my body die away!

My fire is dead: it knew no pain;
Yet is it dead, and I remain.
All stiff with ice the ashes lie;
And they are dead, and I will die.
When I was well, I wished to live,
For clothes, for warmth, for food, and fire;
But they to me no joy can give,
No pleasure now, and no desire.
Then here contented will I lie;
Alone I cannot fear to die.

Alas! you might have dragged me on
Another day, a single one!

Too soon despair o'er me prevailed;
Too soon my heartless spirit failed;
When you were gone my limbs were stronger,
And Oh how grievously I rue,
That, afterwards, a little longer,
My friends, I did not follow you!
For strong and without pain I lay,
My friends, when you were gone away.

My child! they gave thee to another,
A woman who was not thy mother.
When from my arms my babe they took,
On me how strangely did he look!
Through his whole body something ran,
A most strange something did I see;
—As if he strove to be a man,
That he might pull the sledge for me.
And then he stretched his arms, how wild!
Oh mercy! like a little child.

My little joy! my little pride!
In two days more I must have died.
Then do not weep and grieve for me;
I feel I must have died with thee.
Oh wind that o'er my head art flying,
The way my friends their course did bend,
I should not feel the pain of dying,
Could I with thee a message send.
Too soon, my friends, you went away;
For I had many things to say.

I'll follow you across the snow,
You travel heavily and slow:
In spite of all my weary pain,
I'll look upon your tents again.
My fire is dead, and snowy white
The water which beside it stood;
The wolf has come to me to-night,
And he has stolen away my food.
For ever left alone am I,
Then wherefore should I fear to die?

My journey will be shortly run,
I shall not see another sun,

I cannot lift my limbs to know
If they have any life or no.
My poor forsaken child! if I
For once could have thee close to me,
With happy heart I then should die,
And my last thoughts would happy be.
I feel my body die away,
I shall not see another day.

THE LAST OF THE FLOCK.

   In distant countries I have been,
And yet I have not often seen
A healthy man, a man full grown,
Weep in the public roads alone.
But such a one, on English ground,
And in the broad high-way, I met;
Along the broad high-way he came,
His cheeks with tears were wet.
Sturdy he seemed, though he was sad;
And in his arms a lamb he had.

   He saw me, and he turned aside,
As if he wished himself to hide:
Then with his coat he made essay
To wipe those briny tears away.
I follow'd him, and said, "My friend
What ails you? wherefore weep you so?"
—"Shame on me, Sir! this lusty lamb,
He makes my tears to flow.
To-day I fetched him from the rock;
He is the last of all my flock."

   When I was young, a single man,
And after youthful follies ran.
Though little given to care and thought,
Yet, so it was, a ewe I bought;
And other sheep from her I raised,
As healthy sheep as you might see,
And then I married, and was rich
As I could wish to be;
Of sheep I numbered a full score,
And every year increas'd my store.

   Year after year my stock it grew,
And from this one, this single ewe,
Full fifty comely sheep I raised,
As sweet a flock as ever grazed!
Upon the mountain did they feed;
They throve, and we at home did thrive.
—This lusty lamb of all my store

Is all that is alive;
And now I care not if we die,
And perish all of poverty.

Six children, Sir! had I to feed,
Hard labour in a time of need!
My pride was tamed, and in our grief,
I of the parish ask'd relief.
They said I was a wealthy man;
My sheep upon the mountain fed,
And it was fit that thence I took
Whereof to buy us bread:
"Do this; how can we give to you,"
They cried, "what to the poor is due?"

I sold a sheep as they had said,
And bought my little children bread,
And they were healthy with their food;
For me it never did me good.
A woeful time it was for me,
To see the end of all my gains,
The pretty flock which I had reared
With all my care and pains,
To see it melt like snow away!
For me it was a woeful day.

Another still! and still another!
A little lamb, and then its mother!
It was a vein that never stopp'd,
Like blood-drops from my heart they dropp'd.
Till thirty were not left alive
They dwindled, dwindled, one by one,
And I may say that many a time
I wished they all were gone:
They dwindled one by one away;
For me it was a woeful day.

To wicked deeds I was inclined, And
wicked fancies cross'd my mind, And
every man I chanc'd to see,
I thought he knew some ill of me.
No peace, no comfort could I find,
No ease, within doors or without,
And crazily, and wearily

I went my work about.
Oft-times I thought to run away;
For me it was a woeful day.

   Sir! 'twas a precious flock to me,
As dear as my own children be;
For daily with my growing store
I loved my children more and more.
Alas! it was an evil time;
God cursed me in my sore distress,
I prayed, yet every day I thought
I loved my children less;
And every week, and every day,
My flock, it seemed to melt away.

   They dwindled. Sir, sad sight to see!
From ten to five, from five to three,
A lamb, a weather, and a ewe;
And then at last, from three to two;
And of my fifty, yesterday
I had but only one,
And here it lies upon my arm,
Alas! and I have none;
To-day I fetched it from the rock;
It is the last of all my flock.

LINES

Left upon a seat in a YEW-TREE, which stands near the Lake of ESTHWAITE, on a desolate part of the shore, yet commanding a beautiful prospect.

—Nay, Traveller! rest. This lonely yew-tree stands
Far from all human dwelling: what if here
No sparkling rivulet spread the verdant herb;
What if these barren boughs the bee not loves;
Yet, if the wind breathe soft, the curling waves,
That break against the shore, shall lull thy mind
By one soft impulse saved from vacancy.

  —Who he was
That piled these stones, and with the mossy sod
First covered o'er and taught this aged tree
With its dark arms to form a circling bower,
I well remember.—He was one who owned
No common soul. In youth by science nursed
And led by nature into a wild scene
Of lofty hopes, he to the world went forth,
A favored being, knowing no desire
Which genius did not hallow, 'gainst the taint
Of dissolute tongues, and jealousy, and hate
And scorn, against all enemies prepared.
All but neglect. The world, for so it thought,
Owed him no service: he was like a plant
Fair to the sun, the darling of the winds,
But hung with fruit which no one, that passed by,
Regarded, and, his spirit damped at once,
With indignation did he turn away
And with the food of pride sustained his soul
In solitude.—Stranger! these gloomy boughs
Had charms for him; and here he loved to sit,
His only visitants a straggling sheep,
The stone-chat, or the glancing sand-piper;
And on these barren rocks, with juniper,
And heath, and thistle, thinly sprinkled o'er,
Fixing his downcast eye, he many an hour
A morbid pleasure nourished, tracing here

An emblem of his own unfruitful life:
And lifting up his head, he then would gaze
On the more distant scene; how lovely 'tis
Thou seest, and he would gaze till it became
Far lovelier, and his heart could not sustain
The beauty still more beauteous. Nor, that time
When Nature had subdued him to herself
Would he forget those beings, to whose minds,
Warm from the labours of benevolence,
The world, and man himself, appeared a scene
Of kindred loveliness: then he would sigh
With mournful joy, to think that others felt
What he must never feel: and so, lost man!
On visionary views would fancy feed,
Till his eye streamed with tears. In this deep vale
He died, this seat his only monument.

If thou be one whose heart the holy forms
Of young imagination have kept pure,
Stranger! henceforth be warned; and know, that pride,
Howe'er disguised in its own majesty,
Is littleness; that he, who feels contempt
For any living thing, hath faculties
Which he has never used; that thought with him
Is in its infancy. The man, whose eye
Is ever on himself, doth look on one,
The least of nature's works, one who might move
The wise man to that scorn which wisdom holds
Unlawful, ever. O, be wiser thou!
Instructed that true knowledge leads to love,
True dignity abides with him alone
Who, in the silent hour of inward thought,
Can still suspect, and still revere himself,
In lowliness of heart.

THE FOSTER-MOTHER'S TALE.
A Narration in Dramatic Blank Verse.

But that entrance, Mother!

FOSTER-MOTHER.

Can no one hear? It is a perilous tale!

MARIA.

No one.

FOSTER-MOTHER.

My husband's father told it me,
Poor old Leoni!—Angels rest his soul!
He was a woodman, and could fell and saw
With lusty arm. You know that huge round beam
Which props the hanging wall of the old chapel?
Beneath that tree, while yet it was a tree
He found a baby wrapt in mosses, lined
With thistle beards, and such small locks of wool
As hang on brambles. Well, he brought him home,
And reared him at the then Lord Velez' cost.
And so the babe grew up a pretty boy,
A pretty boy, but most unteachable—
And never learnt a prayer, nor told a bead.
But knew the names of birds, and mocked their notes,
And whistled, as he were a bird himself:
And all the autumn 'twas his only play
To get the seeds of wild flowers, and to plant them
With earth and water, on the stumps of trees.
A Friar, who gathered simples in the wood,
A grey-haired man—he loved this little boy,
The boy loved him—and, when the Friar taught him,
He soon could write with the pen: and from that time,
Lived chiefly at the Convent or the Castle.
So he became a very learned youth.
But Oh! poor wretch!—he read, and read, and read,
Till his brain turned—and ere his twentieth year,
He had unlawful thoughts of many things:
And though he prayed, he never loved to pray
With holy men, nor in a holy place—
But yet his speech, it was so soft and sweet,
The late Lord Velez ne'er was wearied with him.
And once, as by the north side of the Chapel
They stood together, chained in deep discourse,
The earth heaved under them with such a groan,
That the wall tottered, and had well-nigh fallen
Right on their heads. My Lord was sorely frightened;

A fever seized him, and he made confession
Of all the heretical and lawless talk
Which brought this judgment: so the youth was seized
And cast into that cell. My husband's father
Sobbed like a child—it almost broke his heart:
And once as he was working in the cellar,
He heard a voice distinctly; 'twas the youth's
Who sang a doleful song about green fields,
How sweet it were on lake or wild savannah,
To hunt for food, and be a naked man,
And wander up and down at liberty.
Leoni doted on the youth, and now
His love grew desperate; and defying death,
He made that cunning entrance I described:
And the young man escaped.

MARIA.

'Tis a sweet tale.
And what became of him?

FOSTER-MOTHER.

He went on ship-board
With those bold voyagers, who made discovery
Of golden lands. Leoni's younger brother
Went likewise, and when he returned to Spain,
He told Leoni, that the poor mad youth,
Soon after they arrived in that new world,
In spite of his dissuasion, seized a boat,
And all alone, set sail by silentmoonlight
Up a great river, great as any sea,
And ne'er was heard of more: but 'tis supposed,
He lived and died among the savage men.

GOODY BLAKE & HARRY GILL,

A TRUE STORY,

Oh! what's the matter? what's the matter?
What is't that ails young Harry Gill?
That evermore his teeth they chatter,

Chatter, chatter, chatter still.
Of waistcoats Harry has no lack,
Good duffle grey, and flannel fine;
He has a blanket on his back,
And coats enough to smother nine.

In March, December, and in July,
'Tis all the same with Harry Gill;
The neighbours tell, and tell you truly,
His teeth they chatter, chatter still.
At night, at morning, and at noon,
'Tis all the same with Harry Gill;
Beneath the sun, beneath the moon,
His teeth they chatter, chatter still.

Young Harry was a lusty drover,
And who so stout of limb as he?
His cheeks were red as ruddy clover,
His voice was like the voice of three.
Auld Goody Blake was old and poor,
Ill fed she was, and thinly clad;
And any man who pass'd her door,
Might see how poor a hut she had.

All day she spun in her poor dwelling,
And then her three hours' work at night!
Alas! 'twas hardly worth the telling,
It would not pay for candle-light.
—This woman dwelt in Dorsetshire,
Her hut was on a cold hill-side,
And in that country coals are dear,
For they come far by wind and tide.

By the same fire to boil their pottage,
Two poor old dames as I have known,
Will often live in one small cottage,
But she, poor woman, dwelt alone.
'Twas well enough when summer came,
The long, warm, lightsome summer-day,
Then at her door the *canty* dame
Would sit, as any linnet gay.

But when the ice our streams did fetter,
Oh! then how her old bones would shake!
You would have said, if you had met her,

'Twas a hard time for Goody Blake.
Her evenings then were dull and dead;
Sad case it was, as you may think,
For very cold to go to bed,
And then for cold not sleep a wink.

  Oh joy for her! whene'er in winter
The winds at night had made a rout,
And scatter'd many a lusty splinter,
And many a rotten bough about.
Yet never had she, well or sick,
As every man who knew her says,
A pile before hand, wood or stick,
Enough to warm her for three days.

  Now when the frost was past enduring,
And made her poor old bones to ache,
Could any thing be more alluring,
Than an old hedge to Goody Blake?
And now and then, it must be said,
When her old bones were cold and chill,
She left her fire, or left her bed,
To seek the hedge of Harry Gill.

  Now Harry he had long suspected
This trespass of old Goody Blake,
And vow'd that she should be detected,
And he on her would vengeance take.
And oft from his warm fire he'd go,
And to the fields his road would take,
And there, at night, in frost and snow,
He watch'd to seize old Goody Blake.

  And once, behind a rick of barley,
Thus looking out did Harry stand;
The moon was full and shining clearly,
And crisp with frost the stubble land.
—He hears a noise—he's all awake—
Again?—on tip-toe down the hill
He softly creeps—'Tis Goody Blake,
She's at the hedge of Harry Gill.

  Right glad was he when he beheld her;
Stick after stick did Goody pull,
He stood behind a bush of elder,

Till she had filled her apron full.
When with her load she turned about,
The bye-road back again to take,
He started forward with a shout, And
sprang upon poor Goody Blake.

And fiercely by the arm he took her,
And by the arm he held her fast,
And fiercely by the arm he shook her,
And cried, "I've caught you then at last!"
Then Goody, who had nothing said,
Her bundle from her lap let fall;
And kneeling on the sticks, she pray'd
To God that is the judge of all.

She pray'd, her wither'd hand uprearing,
While Harry held her by the arm—
"God! who art never out of hearing,
O may he never more be warm!"
The cold, cold moon above her head,
Thus on her knees did Goody pray,
Young Harry heard what she had said;
And icy-cold he turned away.

He went complaining all the morrow
That he was cold and very chill:
His face was gloom, his heart was sorrow,
Alas! that day for Harry Gill!
That day he wore a riding-coat,
But not a whit the warmer he:
Another was on Thursday brought,
And ere the Sabbath he had three.

'Twas all in vain, a useless matter,
And blankets were about him pinn'd;
Yet still his jaws and teeth they clatter,
Like a loose casement in the wind.
And Harry's flesh it fell away;
And all who see him say 'tis plain,
That, live as long as live he may,
He never will be warm again.

No word to any man he utters,
A-bed or up, to young or old;
But ever to himself he mutters,

"Poor Harry Gill is very cold."
A-bed or up, by night or day;
His teeth they chatter, chatter still.
Now think, ye farmers all, I pray,
Of Goody Blake and Harry Gill.

THE THORN.

I.

   There is a thorn; it looks so old,
In truth you'd find it hard to say,
How it could ever have been young,
It looks so old and grey.
Not higher than a two years' child
It stands erect this aged thorn;
No leaves it has, no thorny points;
It is a mass of knotted joints,
A wretched thing forlorn.
It stands erect, and like a stone
With lichens it is overgrown.

II.

   Like rock or stone, it is o'ergrown
With lichens to the very top,
And hung with heavy tufts of moss,
A melancholy crop:
Up from the earth these mosses creep,
And this poor thorn! they clasp it round
So close, you'd say that they were bent
With plain and manifest intent,
To drag it to the ground;
And all had join'd in one endeavour
To bury this poor thorn for ever.

III.

   High on a mountain's highest ridge,
Where oft the stormy winter gale
Cuts like a scythe, while through the clouds
It sweeps from vale to vale;
Not five yards from the mountain-path,
This thorn you on your left espy;

And to the left, three yards beyond,
You see a little muddy pond
Of water, never dry;
I've measured it from side to side:
'Tis three feet long, and two feet wide.

IV.

And close beside this aged thorn,
There is a fresh and lovely sight,
A beauteous heap, a hill of moss,
Just half a foot in height.
All lovely colours there you see,
All colours that were ever seen,
And mossy network too is there,
As if by hand of lady fair
The work had woven been,
And cups, the darlings of the eye,
So deep is their vermillion dye.

V.

Ah me! what lovely tints are there!
Of olive green and scarlet bright,
In spikes, in branches, and in stars,
Green, red, and pearly white.
This heap of earth o'ergrown with moss,
Which close beside the thorn you see,
So fresh in all its beauteous dyes,
Is like an infant's grave in size
As like as like can be:
But never, never any where,
An infant's grave was half so fair.

VI.

Now would you see this aged thorn,
This pond and beauteous hill of moss,
You must take care and chuse your time

The mountain when to cross.
For oft there sits, between the heap
That's like an infant's grave in size
And that same pond of which I spoke,
A woman in a scarlet cloak,
And to herself she cries,
"Oh misery! oh misery!
Oh woe is me! oh misery!"

VII.

 At all times of the day and night
This wretched woman thither goes,
And she is known to every star,
And every wind that blows;
And there beside the thorn she sits
When the blue day-light's in the skies,
And when the whirlwind's on the hill,
Or frosty air is keen and still,
And to herself she cries,
"Oh misery! oh misery!
Oh woe is me! oh misery;"

VIII.

 "Now wherefore thus, by day and night,
In rain, in tempest, and in snow
Thus to the dreary mountain-top
Does this poor woman go?
And why sits she beside the thorn
When the blue day-light's in the sky,
Or when the whirlwind's on the hill,
Or frosty air is keen and still,
And wherefore does she cry?—
Oh wherefore? wherefore? tell me why
Does she repeat that doleful cry?"

IX.

I cannot tell; I wish I could;
For the true reason no one knows,
But if you'd gladly view the spot,
The spot to which she goes;
The heap that's like an infant's grave,
The pond—and thorn, so old and grey.
Pass by her door—tis seldom shut—
And if you see her in her hut,
Then to the spot away!—
I never heard of such as dare
Approach the spot when she is there.

X.

"But wherefore to the mountain-top,
Can this unhappy woman go,
Whatever star is in the skies,
Whatever wind may blow?"
Nay rack your brain—'tis all in vain,
I'll tell you every thing I know;
But to the thorn and to the pond
Which is a little step beyond,
I wish that you would go: Perhaps
when you are at the place
You something of her tale may trace.

XI.

I'll give you the best help I can:
Before you up the mountain go,
Up to the dreary mountain-top,
I'll tell you all I know.
'Tis now some two and twenty years,
Since she (her name is Martha Ray)
Gave with a maiden's true good will
Her company to Stephen Hill;
And she was blithe and gay,
And she was happy, happy still
Whene'er she thought of Stephen Hill.

XII.

And they had fix'd the wedding-day,
The morning that must wed them both;
But Stephen to another maid
Had sworn another oath;
And with this other maid to church
Unthinking Stephen went—
Poor Martha! on that woful day
A cruel, cruel fire, they say,
Into her bones was sent:
It dried her body like a cinder,
And almost turn'd her brain to tinder.

XII.

They say, full six months after this,
While yet the summer leaves were green,
She to the mountain-top would go,
And there was often seen.
'Tis said, a child was in her womb,
As now to any eye was plain;
She was with child, and she was mad,
Yet often she was sober sad
From her exceeding pain.
Oh me! ten thousand times I'd rather,
That he had died, that cruel father!

XIV.

Sad case for such a brain to hold
Communion with a stirring child!
Sad case, as you may think, for one
Who had a brain so wild!
Last Christmas when we talked ofthis,
Old Farmer Simpson did maintain,
That in her womb the infant wrought
About its mother's heart, and brought
Her senses back again:
And when at last her time drew near,

Her looks were calm, her senses clear.

XV.

No more I know, I wish I did,
And I would tell it all to you;
For what became of this poor child
There's none that ever knew:
And if a child was born or no,
There's no one that could ever tell
And if 'twas born alive or dead,
There's no one knows, as I have said,
But some remember well,
That Martha Ray about this time
Would up the mountain often climb.

XVI.

And all that winter, when at night
The wind blew from the mountain-peak,
'Twas worth your while, though in the dark,
The church-yard path to seek:
For many a time and oft were heard
Cries coming from the mountain-head,
Some plainly living voices were,
And others, I've heard many swear,
Were voices of the dead:
I cannot think, whate'er they say,
They had to do with Martha Ray.

XVII.

But that she goes to this old thorn,
The thorn which I've described to you,
And there sits in a scarlet cloak,
I will be sworn is true.
For one day with my telescope,
To view the ocean wide and bright,
When to this country first I came,

Ere I had heard of Martha's name,
I climbed the mountain's height:
A storm came on, and I could see
No object higher than my knee.

XVIII.

'Twas mist and rain, and storm and rain,
No screen, no fence could I discover,
And then the wind! in faith, it was
A wind full ten times over.
Hooked around, I thought I saw
A jutting crag, and off I ran,
Head-foremost, through the driving rain,
The shelter of the crag to gain,
And, as I am a man,
Instead of jutting crag, I found
A woman seated on the ground.

XIX.

I did not speak—I saw her face,
In truth it was enough for me;
I turned about and heard her cry,
"O misery! O misery!"
And there she sits, until the moon
Through half the clear blue sky will go,
And when the little breezes make
The waters of the pond to shake,
As all the country know
She shudders, and you hear her cry,
"Oh misery! oh misery!"

XX.

"But what's the thorn? and what's the pond?
And what's the hill of moss to her?
And what's the creeping breeze that comes
The little pond to stir?"

I cannot tell; but some will say
She hanged her baby on the tree,
Some say she drowned it in the pond,
Which is a little step beyond,
But all and each agree,
The little babe was buried there,
Beneath that hill of moss so fair.

XXI.

   I've heard, the moss is spotted red
With drops of that poor infant's blood;
But kill a new-born infant thus!
I do not think she could.
Some say, if to the pond you go,
And fix on it a steady view,
The shadow of a babe you trace,
A baby and a baby's face,
And that it looks at you;
Whene'er you look on it, 'tis plain
The baby looks at you again.

XXII.

   And some had sworn an oath that she
Should be to public justice brought;
And for the little infant's bones
With spades they would have sought.
But then the beauteous bill of moss
Before their eyes began to stir;
And for full fifty yards around,
The grass it shook upon the ground;
But all do still aver
The little babe is buried there.
Beneath that hill of moss so fair.

XXIII.

   I cannot tell how this may be,

But plain it is, the thorn is bound
With heavy tufts of moss, that strive
To drag it to the ground.
And this I know, full many a time,
When she was on the mountain high,
By day, and in the silent night;
When all the stars shone clear and bright,
That I have heard her cry,
"Oh misery! oh misery!
O woe is me! oh misery!"

WE ARE SEVEN.

A simple child, dear brother Jim,
That lightly draws its breath,
And feels its life in every limb,
What should it know of death?

I met a little cottage girl,
She was eight years old, she said;
Her hair was thick with many a curl
That cluster'd round her head.

She had a rustic, woodland air,
And she was wildly clad;
Her eyes were fair, and very fair,
—Her beauty made me glad.

"Sisters and brothers, little maid,
How many may you be?"
"How many? seven in all," she said,
And wondering looked at me.

"And where are they, I pray you tell?"
She answered, "Seven are we,
And two of us at Conway dwell,
And two are gone to sea."

"Two of us in the church-yard lie,
My sister and my brother,
And in the church-yard cottage, I
Dwell near them with my mother."

"You say that two at Conway dwell,
And two are gone to sea,
Yet you are seven; I pray you tell
Sweet Maid, how this may be?"

Then did the little Maid reply,
"Seven boys and girls are we;
Two of us in the church-yard lie,
Beneath the church-yard tree."

"You run about, my little maid,
Your limbs they are alive;
If two are in the church-yard laid,

Then ye are only five."

"Their graves are green, they may be seen,"
The little Maid replied,
"Twelve steps or more from my mother's door,
And they are side by side."

"My stockings there I often knit,
My 'kerchief there I hem;
And there upon the ground I sit—
I sit and sing to them."

"And often after sunset, Sir,
When it is light and fair,
I take my little porringer,
And eat my supper there."

"The first that died was little Jane;
In bed she moaning lay,
Till God released her of her pain,
And then she went away."

"So in the church-yard she was laid,
And all the summer dry,
Together round her grave we played,
My brother John and I."

"And when the ground was white with snow,
And I could run and slide,
My brother John was forced to go,
And he lies by her side."

"How many are you then," said I,
"If they two are in Heaven?"
The little Maiden did reply,
"O Master! we are seven."

"But they are dead; those two are dead!
Their spirits are in heaven!"
'Twas throwing words away; for still
The little Maid would have her will,
And said, "Nay, we are seven!"

ANECDOTE for FATHERS,
Shewing how the practice of Lying may be taught.

I have a boy of five years old,

His face is fair and fresh to see;
His limbs are cast in beauty's mould,
And dearly he loves me.

One morn we stroll'd on our dry walk,
Our quiet house all full in view,
And held such intermitted talk
As we are wont to do.

My thoughts on former pleasures ran;
I thought of Kilve's delightful shore,
My pleasant home, when Spring began,
A long, long year before.

A day it was when I could bear
To think, and think, and think again;
With so much happiness to spare,
I could not feel a pain.

My boy was by my side, so slim
And graceful in his rustic dress!
And oftentimes I talked to him
In very idleness.

The young lambs ran a pretty race;
The morning sun shone bright and warm;
"Kilve," said I, "was a pleasant place,
And so is Liswyn farm."

"My little boy, which like you more,"
I said and took him by the arm—
"Our home by Kilve's delightful shore,
Or here at Liswyn farm?"

"And tell me, had you rather be,"
I said and held-him by the arm,
"At Kilve's smooth shore by the green sea,
Or here at Liswyn farm?"

In careless mood he looked at me,
While still I held him by the arm,
And said, "At Kilve I'd rather be
Than here at Liswyn farm."

"Now, little Edward, say why so;
My little Edward, tell me why;"
"I cannot tell, I do not know."

"Why this is strange," said I.

"For, here are woods and green hills warm:
There surely must some reason be
Why you would change sweet Liswyn farm,
For Kilve by the green sea."

At this, my boy hung down his head,
He blush'd with shame, nor made reply;
And five times to the child I said,
"Why, Edward, tell me, why?"

His head he raised—there was in sight,
It caught his eye, he saw it plain—
Upon the house-top, glittering bright,
A broad and gilded vane.

Then did the boy his tongue unlock,
And thus to me he made reply;
"At Kilve there was no weather-cock,
And that's the reason why."

Oh dearest, dearest boy! my heart
For better lore would seldom yearn
Could I but teach the hundredth part
Of what from thee I learn.

LINES

*Written at a small distance from my House, and sent by
my little boy to the person to whom they are addressed.*

It is the first mild day of March:
Each minute sweeter than before,
The red-breast sings from the tall larch
That stands beside our door.

There is a blessing in the air,
Which seems a sense of joy to yield
To the bare trees, and mountains bare,
And grass in the green field.

My Sister! ('tis a wish of mine)
Now that our morning meal is done,
Make haste, your morning task resign;
Come forth and feel the sun.

Edward will come with you, and pray,

Put on with speed your woodland dress,
And bring no book, for this one day
We'll give to idleness.

No joyless forms shall regulate
Our living Calendar:
We from to-day, my friend, will date
The opening of the year.

Love, now an universal birth,
From heart to heart is stealing,
From earth to man, from man to earth,
—It is the hour of feeling.

One moment now may give us more
Than fifty years of reason;
Our minds shall drink at every pore
The spirit of the season.

Some silent laws our hearts may make,
Which they shall long obey;
We for the year to come may take
Our temper from to-day.

And from the blessed power that rolls
About, below, above;
We'll frame the measure of our souls,
They shall be tuned to love.

Then come, my sister I come, I pray,
With speed put on your woodland dress,
And bring no book; for this one day
We'll give to idleness.

THE FEMALE VAGRANT

　By Derwent's side my Father's cottage stood,
(The Woman thus her artless story told)
One field, a flock, and what the neighbouring flood
Supplied, to him were more than mines of gold.
Light was my sleep; my days in transport roll'd:
With thoughtless joy I stretch'd along the shore
My father's nets, or from the mountain fold
Saw on the distant lake his twinkling oar
Or watch'd his lazy boat still less'ning more and more

　My father was a good and pious man,
An honest man by honest parents bred,
And I believe that, soon as I began
To lisp, he made me kneel beside my bed,
And in his hearing there my prayers I said:
And afterwards, by my good father taught,
I read, and loved the books in which I read;
For books in every neighbouring house I sought,
And nothing to my mind a sweeter pleasure brought.

　Can I forget what charms did once adorn
My garden, stored with pease, and mint, and thyme,
And rose and lilly for the sabbath morn?
The sabbath bells, and their delightful chime;
The gambols and wild freaks at shearing time;
My hen's rich nest through long grass scarce espied;
The cowslip-gathering at May's dewy prime;
The swans, that, when I sought the water-side,
From far to meet me came, spreading their snowy pride.

　The staff I yet remember which upbore
The bending body of my active sire;
His seat beneath the honeyed sycamore
When the bees hummed, and chair by winter fire;
When market-morning came, the neat attire
With which, though bent on haste, myself I deck'd;
My watchful dog, whose starts of furious ire,
When stranger passed, so often I have check'd;
The red-breast known for years, which at my casement peck'd.

47

The suns of twenty summers danced along,—
Ah! little marked, how fast they rolled away:
Then rose a stately hall our woods among,
And cottage after cottage owned its sway.
No joy to see a neighbouring house, or stray
Through pastures not his own, the master took;
My Father dared his greedy wish gainsay;
He loved his old hereditary nook,
And ill could I the thought of such sad parting brook.

But when he had refused the proffered gold,
To cruel injuries he became a prey,
Sore traversed in whate'er he bought and sold:
His troubles grew upon him day by day,
Till all his substance fell into decay. His
little range of water was denied; [3] All
but the bed where his old body lay.
All, all was seized, and weeping, side by side,
We sought a home where we uninjured might abide.

[Footnote 3: Several of the Lakes in the north of England are let out to
different Fishermen, in parcels marked out by imaginary lines drawn from
rock to rock.]

Can I forget that miserable hour,
When from the last hill-top, my sire surveyed,
Peering above the trees, the steeple tower
That on his marriage-day sweet music made?
Till then he hoped his bones might there be laid,
Close by my mother in their native bowers:
Bidding me trust in God, he stood and prayed,—
I could not pray:—through tears that fell in showers,
Glimmer'd our dear-loved home, alas! no longer ours!

There was a youth whom I had loved so long.
That when I loved him not I cannot say.
'Mid the green mountains many and many a song
We two had sung, like gladsome birds in May.
When we began to tire of childish play
We seemed still more and more to prize each other;
We talked of marriage and our marriage day;
And I in truth did love him like a brother,
For never could I hope to meet with such another.

His father said, that to a distant town

He must repair, to ply the artist's trade.
What tears of bitter grief till then unknown?
What tender vows our last sad kiss delayed!
To him we turned:—we had no other aid.
Like one revived, upon his neck I wept,
And her whom he had loved in joy, he said
He well could love in grief: his faith he kept;
And in a quiet home once more my father slept.

  Four years each day with daily bread was blest,
By constant toil and constant prayer supplied.
Three lovely infants lay upon my breast;
And often, viewing their sweet smiles, I sighed,
And knew not why. My happy father died
When sad distress reduced the childrens' meal:
Thrice happy! that from him the grave did hide
The empty loom, cold hearth, and silent wheel,
And tears that flowed for ills which patience could not heal.

  'Twas a hard change, an evil time was come;
We had no hope, and no relief could gain.
But soon, with proud parade, the noisy drum
Beat round, to sweep the streets of want and pain.
My husband's arms now only served to strain
Me and his children hungering in his view:
In such dismay my prayers and tears were vain:
To join those miserable men he flew;
And now to the sea-coast, with numbers more, we drew.

  There foul neglect for months and months we bore,
Nor yet the crowded fleet its anchor stirred.
Green fields before us and our native shore,
By fever, from polluted air incurred,
Ravage was made, for which no knell was heard.
Fondly we wished, and wished away, nor knew,
'Mid that long sickness, and those hopes deferr'd,
That happier days we never more must view:
The parting signal streamed, at last the land withdrew.

  But from delay the summer calms were past.
On as we drove, the equinoctial deep
Ran mountains-high before the howling blast.
We gazed with terror on the gloomy sleep
Of them that perished in the whirlwind's sweep,

Untaught that soon such anguish must ensue,
Our hopes such harvest of affliction reap,
That we the mercy of the waves should rue.
We readied the western world, a poor, devoted crew.

  Oh I dreadful price of being to resign
All that is dear *in* being! better far
In Want's most lonely cave till death to pine,
Unseen, unheard, unwatched by any star;
Or in the streets and walks where proud men are,
Better our dying bodies to obtrude,
Than dog-like, wading at the heels of war,
Protract a curst existence, with the brood
That lap (their very nourishment!) their brother's blood.

  The pains and plagues that on our heads came down;
Disease and famine, agony and fear,
In wood or wilderness, in camp or town,
It would thy brain unsettle even to hear.
All perished—all, in one remorseless year,
Husband and children! one by one, by sword
And ravenous plague, all perished: every tear
Dried up, despairing, desolate, on board
A British ship I waked, as from a trance restored.

  Peaceful as some immeasurable plain
By the first beams of dawning light impress'd;
In the calm sunshine slept the glittering main,
The very ocean has its hour of rest,
That comes not to the human mourner's breast.
Remote from man, and storms of mortal care,
A heavenly silence did the waves invest:
I looked and looked along the silent air,
Until it seemed to bring a joy to my despair.

  Ah! how unlike those late terrific sleeps!
And groans, that rage of racking famine spoke:
The unburied dead that lay in festering heaps!
The breathing pestilence that rose like smoke!
The shriek that from the distant battle broke!
The mine's dire earthquake, and the pallid host
Driven by the bomb's incessant thunder-stroke
To loathsome vaults, where heart-sick anguish toss'd,
Hope died, and fear itself in agony was lost!

Yet does that burst of woe congeal my frame,
When the dark streets appeared to heave and gape,
While like a sea the storming army came,
And Fire from hell reared his gigantic shape,
And Murder, by the ghastly gleam, and Rape
Seized their joint prey, the mother and the child!
But from these crazing thoughts my brain, escape!
—For weeks the balmy air breathed soft and mild,
And on the gliding vessel Heaven and Ocean smiled.

Some mighty gulph of separation past,
I seemed transported to another world:—
A thought resigned with pain, when from the mast
The impatient mariner the sail unfurl'd,
And whistling, called the wind that hardly curled
The silent sea. From the sweet thoughts of home,
And from all hope I was forever hurled.
For me—farthest from earthly port to roam
Was best, could I but shun the spot where man might
    come.

And oft, robb'd of my perfect mind, I thought
At last my feet a resting-place had found:
Here will I weep in peace, (so fancy wrought,)
Roaming the illimitable waters round;
Here watch, of every human friend disowned,
All day, my ready tomb the ocean-flood—
To break my dream the vessel reached its bound:
And homeless near a thousand homes I stood,
And near a thousand tables pined, and wanted food.

By grief enfeebled was I turned adrift,
Helpless as sailor cast on desert rock;
Nor morsel to my mouth that day did lift,
Nor dared my hand at any door to knock.
I lay, where with his drowsy mates, the cock
From the cross timber of an out-house hung;
How dismal tolled, that night, the city clock!
At morn my sick heart hunger scarcely stung,
Nor to the beggar's language could I frame my tongue.

So passed another day, and so the third:
Then did I try, in vain, the crowd's resort,
In deep despair by frightful wishes stirr'd,

Near the sea-side I reached a ruined fort:
There, pains which nature could no more support,
With blindness linked, did on my vitals fall;
Dizzy my brain, with interruption short
Of hideous sense; I sunk, nor step could crawl,
And thence was borne away to neighbouring hospital.

Recovery came with food: but still, my brain
Was weak, nor of the past had memory.
I heard my neighbours, in their beds, complain
Of many things which never troubled me;
Of feet still bustling round with busy glee,
Of looks where common kindness had no part.
Of service done with careless cruelty,
Fretting the fever round the languid heart,
And groans, which, as they said, would make a dead man start.

These things just served to stir the torpid sense,
Nor pain nor pity in my bosom raised.
Memory, though slow, returned with strength: and thence
Dismissed, again on open day I gazed,
At houses, men, and common light, amazed.
The lanes I sought, and as the sun retired,
Came, where beneath the trees a faggot blazed;
The wild brood saw me weep, my fate enquired,
And gave me food, and rest, more welcome, more desired.

My heart is touched to think that men like these,
The rude earth's tenants, were my first relief:
How kindly did they paint their vagrant ease!
And their long holiday that feared not grief,
For all belonged to all, and each was chief.
No plough their sinews strained; on grating road
No wain they drove, and yet, the yellow sheaf
In every vale for their delight was stowed:
For them, in nature's meads, the milky udder flowed,

Semblance, with straw and panniered ass, they made
Of potters wandering on from door to door:
But life of happier sort to me pourtrayed,
And other joys my fancy to allure;
The bag-pipe dinning on the midnight moor
In barn uplighted, and companions boon
Well met from far with revelry secure,

In depth of forest glade, when jocund June
Rolled fast along the sky his warm and genial moon.

  But ill it suited me, in journey dark
O'er moor and mountain, midnight theft to hatch;
To charm the surly house-dog's faithful bark,
Or hang on tiptoe at the lifted latch;
The gloomy lantern, and the dim blue match,
The black disguise, the warning whistle shrill,
And ear still busy on its nightly watch,
Were not for me, brought up in nothing ill;
Besides, on griefs so fresh my thoughts were brooding still.

  What could I do, unaided and unblest?
Poor Father! gone was every friend of thine:
And kindred of dead husband are at best
Small help, and, after marriage such as mine,
With little kindness would to me incline.
Ill was I then for toil or service fit:
With tears whose course no effort could confine,
By high-way side forgetful would I sit
Whole hours, my idle arms in moping sorrow knit.

  I lived upon the mercy of the fields
And oft of cruelty the sky accused;
On hazard, or what general bounty yields.
Now coldly given, now utterly refused,
The fields I for my bed have often used:
But, what afflicts my peace with keenest ruth
Is, that I have my inner self abused,
Foregone the home delight of constant truth,
And clear and open soul, so prized in fearless youth.

  Three years a wanderer, often have I view'd,
In tears, the sun towards that country tend
Where my poor heart lost all its fortitude:
And now across this moor my steps I bend—
Oh! tell me whither—for no earthly friend
Have I.—She ceased, and weeping turned away,
As if because her tale was at an end
She wept;—because she had no more to say
Of that perpetual weight which on her spirit lay.

THE DUNGEON.

And this place our forefathers made for man!
This is the process of our love and wisdom
To each poor brother who offends against us—
Most innocent, perhaps—and what if guilty?
Is this the only cure? Merciful God!
Each pore and natural outlet shrivell'd up
By ignorance and parching poverty,
His energies roll back upon his heart,
And stagnate and corrupt; till changed to poison,
They break out on him, like a loathsome plague spot.
Then we call in our pamper'd mountebanks—
And this is their best cure! uncomforted.

And friendless solitude, groaning and tears.
And savage faces, at the clanking hour,
Seen through the steams and vapour of his dungeon,
By the lamp's dismal twilight! So he lies
Circled with evil, till his very soul
Unmoulds its essence, hopelessly deformed
By sights of ever more deformity!

With other ministrations thou, O nature!'
Healest thy wandering and distempered child:
Thou pourest on him thy soft influences.
Thy sunny hues, fair forms, and breathing sheets,
Thy melodies of woods, and winds, and waters,
Till he relent, and can no more endure
To be a jarring and a dissonant thing,
Amid this general dance and minstrelsy;
But, bursting into tears, wins back his way,
His angry spirit healed and harmonized
By the benignant touch of love and beauty.

SIMON LEE, THE OLD HUNTSMAN,
  With an incident in which he was concerned.

In the sweet shire of Cardigan,
Not far from pleasant Ivor-hall,
An old man dwells, a little man,
I've heard he once was tall.

Of years he has upon his back,
No doubt, a burthen weighty;
He says he is three score and ten,
But others say he's eighty.

  A long blue livery-coat has he,
That's fair behind, and fair before;
Yet, meet him where you will, you see
At once that he is poor.
Full five and twenty years he lived
A running huntsman merry;
And, though he has but one eye left,
His cheek is like a cherry.

  No man like him the horn could sound,
And no man was so full of glee;
To say the least, four counties round.
Had heard of Simon Lee;
His master's dead, and no one now
Dwells in the hall of Ivor;
Men, dogs, and horses, all are dead;
He is the sole survivor.

  His hunting feats have him bereft
Of his right eye, as you may see:
And then, what limbs those feats have left
To poor old Simon Lee!
He has no son, he has no child,
His wife, an aged woman,
Lives with him, near the waterfall,
Upon the village common.

  And he is lean and he is sick,
His dwindled body's half awry,
His ancles they are swoln and thick;
His legs are thin and dry.
When he was young he little knew
'Of husbandry or tillage;
And now he's forced to work, though weak,
—The weakest in the village.

  He all the country could outrun,
Could leave both man and horse behind;
And often, ere the race was done,
He reeled and was stone-blind.

And still there's something in the world
At which his heart rejoices;
For when the chiming bounds are out,
He dearly loves their voices!

Old Ruth works out of doors with him.
And does what Simon cannot do;
For she, not over stout of limb,
Is stouter of the two.
And though you with your utmost skill
From labour could not wean them,
Alas! 'tis very little, all
Which they can do between them.

Beside their moss-grown hut of clay,
Not twenty paces from the door,
A scrap of land they have, but they
Are poorest of the poor.
This scrap of land he from the heath
Enclosed when he was stronger;
But what avails the land to them,
Which they can till no longer?

Few months of life has he in store,
As he to you will-tell,
For still, the more he works, the more
His poor old ancles swell.
My gentle reader, I perceive
How patiently you've waited,
And I'm afraid that you expect
Some tale will be related.

O reader! had you in your mind
Such stores as silent thought can bring,
O gentle reader! you would find
A tale in every thing.
What more I have to say is short,
I hope you'll kindly take it;
It is no tale; but should you think,
Perhaps a tale you'll make it.

One summer-day I chanced to see
This old man doing all he could
About the root of an old tree,
A stump of rotten wood.

The mattock totter'd in his hand;
So vain was his endeavour
That at the root of the old tree
He might have worked for ever.

   "You've overtasked, good Simon Lee,
Give me your tool" to him I said;
And at the word right gladly he
Received my proffer'd aid.
I struck, and with a single blow
The tangled root I sever'd,
At which the poor old man so long
And vainly had endeavoured.

   The tears into his eyes were brought,
And thanks and praises seemed to run
So fast out of his heart, I thought
They never would have done.
—I've heard of hearts unkind, kind deeds
With coldness still returning.
Alas! the gratitude of men
Has oftner left me mourning.

LINES
   Written in early Spring.

   I heard a thousand blended notes,
While in a grove I sate reclined,
In that sweet mood when pleasantthoughts
Bring sad thoughts to the mind.

   To her fair works did nature link
The human soul that through me ran;
And much it griev'd my heart to think
What man has made of man.

   Through primrose tufts, in that sweetbower,
The periwinkle trail'd its wreathes;
And 'tis my faith that every flower
Enjoys the air it breathes.

   The birds around me hopp'd and play'd:
Their thoughts I cannot measure,
But the least motion which they made,
It seem'd a thrill of pleasure.

The budding twigs spread out their fan,
To catch the breezy air;
And I must think, do all I can,
That there was pleasure there.

If I these thoughts may not prevent,
If such be of my creed the plan,
Have I not reason to lament
What man has made of man?

The NIGHTINGALE.
Written in April, 1798.

No cloud, no relique of the sunken day
Distinguishes the West, no long thin slip
Of sullen Light, no obscure trembling hues.
Come, we will rest on this old mossy Bridge!
You see the glimmer of the stream beneath,
But hear no murmuring: it flows silently
O'er its soft bed of verdure. All is still,
A balmy night! and tho' the stars be dim,
Yet let us think upon the vernal showers
That gladden the green earth, and we shall find
A pleasure in the dimness of the stars.

And hark! the Nightingale begins its song
"Most musical, most melancholy" [4] Bird!
A melancholy Bird? O idle thought!
In nature there is nothing melancholy.
—But some night wandering Man, whose heart was pierc'd
With the remembrance of a grievous wrong,
Or slow distemper or neglected love,
(And so, poor Wretch! fill'd all things with himself
And made all gentle sounds tell back the tale
Of his own sorrows) he and such as he
First named these notes a melancholy strain:
And many a poet echoes the conceit;
Poet, who hath been building up the rhyme

[Footnote 4: "*Most musical, most melancholy.*" This passage in Milton
possesses an excellence far superior to that of mere description: it is spoken in
the character of the melancholy Man, and has therefore a *dramatic* propriety.
The Author makes this remark, to rescue himself from the charge of having
alluded with levity to a line in Milton: a charge than which none could be
more painful to him, except perhaps that of having ridiculed his Bible.]

When he had better far have stretch'd his limbs
Beside a 'brook in mossy forest-dell
By sun or moonlight, to the influxes
Of shapes and sounds and shifting elements
Surrendering his whole spirit, of his song
And of his fame forgetful! so his fame
Should share in nature's immortality,
A venerable thing! and so his song
Should make all nature lovelier, and itself
Be lov'd, like nature!—But 'twill not be so;
And youths and maidens most poetical
Who lose the deep'ning twilights of the spring
In ball-rooms and hot theatres, they still
Full of meek sympathy must heave their sighs
O'er Philomela's pity-pleading strains.
My Friend, and my Friend's Sister! we have learnt
A different lore: we may not thus profane
Nature's sweet voices always full of love
And joyance! Tis the merry Nightingale

That crowds, and hurries, and precipitates
With fast thick warble his delicious notes,
As he were fearful, that an April night
Would be too short for him to utter forth
Hi? love-chant, and disburthen his full soul
Of all its music! And I know a grove
Of large extent, hard by a castle huge
Which the great lord inhabits not: and so
This grove is wild with tangling underwood,
And the trim walks are broken up, and grass,
Thin grass and king-cups grow within the paths.
But never elsewhere in one place I knew
So many Nightingales: and far and near
In wood and thicket over the wide grove
They answer and provoke each other's songs—
With skirmish and capricious passagings,
And murmurs musical and swift jug jug
And one low piping sound more sweet than all—
Stirring the air with such an harmony,
That should you close your eyes, you might almost
Forget it was not day!

A most gentle maid

Who dwelleth in her hospitable home
Hard by the Castle, and at latest eve,
(Even like a Lady vow'd and dedicate
To something more than nature in the grove)
Glides thro' the pathways; she knows all their notes,
That gentle Maid! and oft, a moment's space,
What time the moon was lost behind a cloud,
Hath heard a pause of silence: till the Moon
Emerging, hath awaken'd earth and sky
With one sensation, and those wakeful Birds
Have all burst forth in choral minstrelsy,
At if one quick and sudden Gale had swept
An hundred airy harps! And she hath watch'd
Many a Nightingale perch giddily
On blosmy twig still swinging from the breeze,
And to that motion tune his wanton song,
Like tipsy Joy that reels with tossing head.

  Farewell, O Warbler! till to-morrow eve,
And you, my friends! farewell, a short farewell!
We have been loitering long and pleasantly,
And now for our dear homes.—That strain again!
Full fain it would delay me!-My dear Babe,
Who, capable of no articulate sound,
Mars all things with his imitative lisp,
How he would place his hand beside his ear,
His little hand, the small forefinger up,
And bid us listen! And I deem it wise
To make him Nature's playmate. He knows well
The evening star: and once when he awoke
In most distressful mood (some inward pain
Had made up that strange thing, an infant's dream)
I hurried with him to our orchard plot,
And he beholds the moon, and hush'd at once
Suspends his sobs, and laughs most silently,
While his fair eyes that swam with undropt tears
Did glitter in the yellow moon-beam! Well—
It is a father's tale. But if that Heaven
Should give me life, his childhood shall grow up
Familiar with these songs, that with the night
He may associate Joy! Once more farewell,
Sweet Nightingale! once more, my friends! farewell.

LINES
Written when sailing in a Boat At EVENING.

How rich the wave, in front, imprest
With evening twilights summer hues,
While, facing thus the crimson west,
The boat her silent path pursues!
And see how dark the backward stream!
A little moment past, so smiling!
And still, perhaps, with faithless gleam,
Some other loiterer beguiling.

Such views the youthful bard allure,
But, heedless of the following gloom,
He deems their colours shall endure
'Till peace go with him to the tomb.
—And let him nurse his fond deceit,
And what if he must die in sorrow!
Who would not cherish dreams so sweet,
Though grief and pain may come to-morrow?

LINES
Written near Richmond upon the Thames.

Glide gently, thus for ever glide,
O Thames! that other bards may see,
As lovely visions by thy side
As now, fair river! come to me.
Oh glide, fair stream! for ever so;
Thy quiet soul on all bestowing,
'Till all our minds for ever flow,
As thy deep waters now are flowing.

Vain thought! yet be as now thou art,
That in thy waters may be seen
The image of a poet's heart,
How bright, how solemn, how serene!
Such as did once the poet bless,
Who, pouring here a *later* ditty,
Could find no refuge from distress,
But in the milder grief of pity.

Remembrance! as we float along,
For him suspend the dashing oar,
And pray that never child of Song

May know his freezing sorrows more.
How calm! how still! the only sound,
The dripping of the oar suspended!
—The evening darkness gathers round
By virtue's holiest powers attended. [5]

[Footnote 5: Collins's Ode on the death of Thomson, the last written,
I believe, of the poems which were published during his life-time.
This Ode is also alluded to in the next stanza.]

THE IDIOT BOY.

The IDIOT BOY.

'Tis eight o'clock,—a clear March night,
The moon is up—the sky is blue,
The owlet in the moonlight air,
He shouts from nobody knows where;
He lengthens out his lonely shout,
Halloo! halloo! a long halloo!

—Why bustle thus about your door,
What means this bustle, Betty Foy?
Why are you in this mighty fret?
And why on horseback have you set
Him whom you love, your idiot boy?

Beneath the moon that shines so bright,
Till she is tired, let Betty Foy
With girt and stirrup fiddle-faddle;
But wherefore set upon a saddle
Him whom she loves, her idiot boy?

There's scarce a soul that's out of bed;
Good Betty put him down again;
His lips with joy they burr at you,
But, Betty! what has he to do
With stirrup, saddle, or with rein?

The world will say 'tis very idle,
Bethink you of the time of night;
There's not a mother, no not one,
But when she hears what you have done,
Oh! Betty she'll be in a fright.

But Betty's bent on her intent,
For her good neighbour, SusanGale,
Old Susan, she who dwells alone,
Is sick, and makes a piteous moan,
As if her very life would fail.

There's not a house within a mile,
No hand to help them in distress;
Old Susan lies a bed in pain,

63

And sorely puzzled are the twain,
For what she ails they cannot guess.

And Betty's husband's at the wood,
Where by the week he doth abide,
A woodman in the distant vale;
There's none to help poor Susan Gale,
What must be done? what will betide?

And Betty from the lane has fetched
Her pony, that is mild and good,
Whether he be in joy or pain,
Feeding at will along the lane,
Or bringing faggots from the wood.

And he is all in travelling trim,
And by the moonlight, Betty Foy
Has up upon the saddle set,
The like was never heard of yet,
Him whom she loves, her idiot boy.

And he must post without delay
Across the bridge that's in the dale,
And by the church, and o'er the down,
To bring a doctor from the town,
Or she will die, old Susan Gale.

There is no need of boot or spur,
There is no need of whip or wand,
For Johnny has his holly-bough,
And with a hurly-burly now
He shakes the green bough in his hand.

And Betty o'er and o'er has told
The boy who is her best delight,
Both what to follow, what to shun,
What do, and what to leave undone,
How turn to left, and how to right.

And Betty's most especial charge,
Was, "Johnny! Johnny! mind that you
Come home again, nor stop at all,
Come home again, whate'er befal,
My Johnny do, I pray you do."

To this did Johnny answer make,

Both with his head, and with his hand,
And proudly shook the bridle too,
And then! his words were not a few,
Which Betty well could understand.

And now that Johnny is just going,
Though Betty's in a mighty flurry,
She gently pats the pony's side,
On which her idiot boy must ride,
And seems no longer in a hurry.

But when the pony moved his legs,
Oh! then for the poor idiot boy!
For joy he cannot hold the bridle,
For joy his head and heels are idle,
He's idle all for very joy.

And while the pony moves his legs,
In Johnny's left hand you may see,
The green bough's motionless and dead:
The moon that shines above his head
Is not more still and mute than he.

His heart it was so full of glee,
That till full fifty yards were gone,
He quite forgot his holly whip,
And all his skill in horsemanship,
Oh! happy, happy, happy John.

And Betty's standing at the door,
And Betty's face with joy o'erflows,
Proud of herself, and proud of him,
She sees him in his travelling trim;
How quietly her Johnny goes.

The silence of her idiot boy,
What hopes it sends to Betty's heart!
He's at the guide-post—he turns right,
She watches till he's out of sight,
And Betty will not then depart.

Burr, burr—now Johnny's lips they burr,
As loud as any mill, or near it,
Meek as a lamb the pony moves,
And Johnny makes the noise he loves,
And Betty listens, glad to hear it.

Away she hies to Susan Gale:
And Johnny's in a merry tune,
The owlets hoot, the owlets purr,
And Johnny's lips they burr, burr, burr,
And on he goes beneath the moon.

His steed and he right well agree,
For of this pony there's a rumour,
That should he lose his eyes and ears,
And should he live a thousand years,
He never will be out of humour.

But then he is a horse that thinks!
And when he thinks his pace is slack;
Now, though he knows poor Johnny well,
Yet for his life he cannot tell
What he has got upon his back.

So through the moonlight lanes they go,
And far into the moonlight dale,
And by the church, and o'er the down,
To bring a doctor from the town,
To comfort poor old Susan Gale.

And Betty, now at Susan's side,
Is in the middle of her story,
What comfort Johnny soon will bring,
With many a most diverting thing,
Of Johnny's wit and Johnny's glory.

And Betty's still at Susan's side:
By this time she's not quite so flurried;
Demure with porringer and plate
She sits, as if in Susan's fate
Her life and soul were buried.

But Betty, poor good woman! she,
You plainly in her face may read it,
Could lend out of that moment's store
Five years of happiness or more,
To any that might need it.

But yet I guess that now and then
With Betty all was not so well,
And to the road she turns her ears,
And thence full many a sound she hears,

Which she to Susan will not tell.

Poor Susan moans, poor Susan groans,
"As sure as there's a moon in heaven,"
Cries Betty, "he'll be back again;
They'll both be here, 'tis almost ten,
They'll both be here before eleven."

Poor Susan moans, poor Susan groans,
The clock gives warning for eleven;
'Tis on the stroke—"If Johnny's near,"
Quoth Betty "he will soon be here,
As sure as there's a moon in heaven."

The clock is on the stroke of twelve,
And Johnny is not yet in sight,
The moon's in heaven, as Betty sees,
But Betty is not quite at ease;
And Susan has a dreadful night.

And Betty, half an hour ago,
On Johnny vile reflections cast:
"A little idle sauntering thing!"
With other names, an endless string.
But now that time is gone and past.

And Betty's drooping at the heart.
That happy time all past and gone,
"How can it be he is so late?
The Doctor he has made him wait,
Susan! they'll both be here anon."

And Susan's growing worse and worse,
And Betty's in a sad quandary;
And then there's nobody to say
If she must go or she must stay:
—She's in a sad quandary.

The clock is on the stroke of one;
But neither Doctor nor his guide
Appear along the moonlight road,
There's neither horse nor man abroad,
And Betty's still at Susan's side.

And Susan she begins to fear
Of sad mischances not a few,

That Johnny may perhaps be drown'd,
Or lost perhaps, and never found;
Which they must both for ever rue.

  She prefaced half a hint of this
With, "God forbid it should be true!"
At the first word that Susan said
Cried Betty, rising from the bed,
"Susan, I'd gladly stay with you."

  "I must be gone, I must away,
Consider, Johnny's but half-wise;
Susan, we must take care of him,
If he is hurt in life or limb"—
"Oh God forbid!" poor Susan cries.

  "What can I do?" says Betty, going,
"What can I do to ease your pain?
Good Susan tell me, and I'll stay;
I fear you're in a dreadful way,
But I shall soon be back again."

  "Nay, Betty, go! good Betty, go!
There's nothing that can ease my pain."
Then off she hies, but with a prayer
That God poor Susan's life would spare,
Till she comes back again.

  So, through the moonlight lane she goes,
And far into the moonlight dale;
And how she ran, and how she walked,
And all that to herself she talked,
Would surely be a tedious tale.

In high and low, above, below,
In great and small, in round and square,
In tree and tower was Johnny seen,
In bush and brake, in black and green,
'Twas Johnny, Johnny, every where.

She's past the bridge that's in the dale,
And now the thought torments her sore,
Johnny perhaps his horse forsook,
To hunt the moon that's in the brook,
And never will be heard of more.

And now she's high upon the down,
Alone amid a prospect wide;
There's neither Johnny nor his horse,
Among the fern or in the gorse;
There's neither doctor nor his guide.

"Oh saints! what is become of him?
Perhaps he's climbed into an oak,
Where he will stay till he is dead;
Or sadly he has been misled,
And joined the wandering gypsey-folk."

"Or him that wicked pony's carried
To the dark cave, the goblins' hall,
Or in the castle he's pursuing,
Among the ghosts, his own undoing;
Or playing with the waterfall,"

At poor old Susan then she railed,
While to the town she posts away;
"If Susan had not been so ill,
Alas! I should have had him still,
My Johnny, till my dying day."

Poor Betty! in this sad distemper,
The doctor's self would hardly spare,
Unworthy things she talked and wild,
Even he, of cattle the most mild,
The pony had his share.

And now she's got into the town,
And to the doctor's door she hies;
'Tis silence all on every side;
The town so long, the town so wide,

Is silent as the skies.

And now she's at the doctor's door,
She lifts the knocker, rap, rap, rap,
The doctor at the casement shews,
His glimmering eyes that peep and doze;
And one hand rubs his old night-cap.

"Oh Doctor! Doctor! where's my Johnny?"
"I'm here, what is't you want with me?"
"Oh Sir! you know I'm Betty Foy,
And I have lost my poor dear boy,
You know him—him you often see;"

"He's not so wise as some folks be,"
"The devil take his wisdom!" said
The Doctor, looking somewhat grim,
"What, woman! should I know of him?"
And, grumbling, he went back to bed.

"O woe is me! O woe is me!
Here will I die; here will I die;
I thought to find my Johnny here,
But he is neither far nor near,
Oh! what a wretched mother I!"

She stops, she stands, she looks about,
Which way to turn she cannot tell.
Poor Betty! it would ease her pain
If she had heart to knock again;
—The clock strikes three—a dismal knell!

Then up along the town she hies,
No wonder if her senses fail,
This piteous news so much it shock'd her,
She quite forgot to send the Doctor,
To comfort poor old Susan Gale.

And now she's high upon the down,
And she can see a mile of road,
"Oh cruel! I'm almost three-score;
Such night as this was ne'er before,
There's not a single soul abroad."

She listens, but she cannot hear
The foot of horse, the voice of man;

The streams with softest sound are flowing,
The grass you almost hear it growing,
You hear it now if e'er you can.

  The owlets through the long blue night
Are shouting to each other still:
Fond lovers, yet not quite hob nob,
They lengthen out the tremulous sob,
That echoes far from hill to hill.

  Poor Betty now has lost all hope,
Her thoughts are bent on deadly sin;
A green-grown pond she just has pass'd,
And from the brink she hurries fast, Lest
she should drown herself therein.

  And now she sits her down and weeps;
Such tears she never shed before;
"Oh dear, dear pony! my sweet joy!
Oh carry back my idiot boy!
And we will ne'er o'erload thee more."

  A thought it come into her head;
"The pony he is mild and good,
And we have always used him well;
Perhaps he's gone along the dell,
And carried Johnny to the wood."

  Then up she springs as if on wings;
She thinks no more of deadly sin;
If Betty fifty ponds should see,
The last of all her thoughts would be,
To drown herself therein.

  Oh reader! now that I might tell
What Johnny and his horse are doing!
What they've been doing all this time,
Oh could I put it into rhyme,
A most delightful tale pursuing!

  Perhaps, and no unlikely thought!
He with his pony now doth roam
The cliffs and peaks so high that are,
To lay his hands upon a star,
And in his pocket bring it home.

Perhaps he's turned himself about,
His face unto his horse's tail,
And still and mute, in wonder lost,
All like a silent horse-man ghost,
He travels on along the vale.

And now, perhaps, he's hunting sheep,
A fierce and dreadful hunter he!
Yon valley, that's so trim and green,
In five months' time, should he be seen,
A desert wilderness will be.

Perhaps, with head and heels on fire,
And like the very soul of evil,
He's galloping away, away,
And so he'll gallop on for aye,
The bane of all that dread the devil.

I to the muses have been bound
These fourteen years, by strong indentures:
Oh gentle muses! let me tell
But half of what to him befel,
For sure he met with strange adventures.

Oh gentle muses! is this kind
Why will ye thus my suit repel?
Why of your further aid bereave me?
And can ye thus unfriended leave me?
Ye muses! whom I love so well.

Who's yon, that, near the waterfall,
Which thunders down with headlong force,
Beneath the moon, yet shining fair,
As careless as if nothing were,
Sits upright on a feeding horse?

Unto his horse, that's feeding free,
He seems, I think, the rein to give;
Of moon or stars he takes no heed;
Of such we in romances read,
—Tis Johnny! Johnny! as I live.

And that's the very pony too.
Where is she, where is Betty Foy?
She hardly can sustain her fears;
The roaring water-fall she hears,

And cannot find her idiot boy.

  Your pony's worth his weight in gold,
Then calm your terrors, Betty Foy!
She's coming from among the trees,
And now all full in view she sees
Him whom she loves, her idiot boy.

  And Betty sees the pony too:
Why stand you thus Good Betty Foy?
It is no goblin, 'tis no ghost,
'Tis he whom you so long have lost,
He whom you love, your idiot boy.

  She looks again-her arms are up—
She screams—she cannot move for joy;
She darts as with a torrent's force,
She almost has o'erturned the horse,
And fast she holds her idiot boy.

  And Johnny burrs, and laughs aloud,
Whether in cunning or in joy,
I cannot tell; but while he laughs,
Betty a drunken pleasure quaffs,
To hear again her idiot boy.

  And now she's at the pony's tail,
And now she's at the pony's head,
On that side now, and now on this,
And almost stifled with her bliss,
A few sad tears does Betty shed.

  She kisses o'er and o'er again,
Him whom she loves, her idiot boy,
She's happy here, she's happy there.
She is uneasy every where;
Her limbs are all alive with joy.

  She pats the pony, where or when
She knows not, happy Betty Foy!
The little pony glad may be,
But he is milder far than she,
You hardly can perceive his joy.

  "Oh! Johnny, never mind the Doctor;
You've done your best, and that is all."

She took the reins, when this was said,
And gently turned the pony's head
From the loud water-fall.

  By this the stars were almost gone,
The moon was setting on the hill,
So pale you scarcely looked at her:
The little birds began to stir,
Though yet their tongues were still.

  The pony, Betty, and her boy,
Wind slowly through the woody dale;
And who is she, be-times abroad,
That hobbles up the steep rough road?
Who is it, but old Susan Gale?

  Long Susan lay deep lost in thought,
And many dreadful fears beset her,
Both for her messenger and nurse;
And as her mind grew worse and worse,
Her body it grew better.

  She turned, she toss'd herself in bed,
On all sides doubts and terrors met her;
Point after point did she discuss;
And while her mind was fighting thus,
Her body still grew better.

  "Alas! what is become of them?
These fears can never be endured,
I'll to the wood."—The word scarce said,
Did Susan rise up from her bed,
As if by magic cured.

  Away she posts up hill and down,
And to the wood at length is come,
She spies her friends, she shouts a greeting;
Oh me! it is a merry meeting,
As ever was in Christendom.

  The owls have hardly sung their last,
While our four travellers homeward wend;
The owls have hooted all night long,
And with the owls began my song,
And with the owls must end.

For while they all were travelling home,
Cried Betty, "Tell us Johnny, do,
Where all this long night you have been,
What you have heard, what you have seen,
And Johnny, mind you tell us true."

Now Johnny all night long had heard
The owls in tuneful concert strive;
No doubt too he the moon had seen;
For in the moonlight he had been
From eight o'clock till five.

And thus to Betty's question, he,
Made answer, like a traveller bold,
(His very words I give to you,)
"The cocks did crow to-whoo, to-whoo,
And the sun did shine so cold."
—Thus answered Johnny in his glory,
And that was all his travel's story.

LOVE.

All Thoughts, all Passions, allDelights,
Whatever stirs this mortal Frame,
All are but Ministers of Love,
  And feed his sacred flame.

Oft in my waking dreams do I
Live o'er again that happy hour,
When midway on the Mount I lay
Beside the Ruin'd Tower.

The Moonshine stealing o'er the scene
Had blended with the Lights of Eve;
And she was there, my Hope, my Joy,
My own dear Genevieve!

She lean'd against the Armed Man,
The Statue of the Armed Knight:
She stood and listen'd to my Harp
Amid the ling'ring Light.

Few Sorrows hath she of her own,
My Hope, my Joy, my Genevieve!
She loves me best, whene'er I sing
The Songs, that make her grieve.

I play'd a soft and doleful Air,
I sang an old and moving Story—
An old rude Song that fitted well
The Ruin wild and hoary.

She listen'd with a flitting Blush,
With downcast Eyes and modestGrace;
For well she knew, I could not choose
But gaze upon her Face.

I told her of the Knight, that wore
Upon his Shield a burning Brand;
And that for ten long Years he woo'd
The Lady of the Land.

I told her, how he pin'd: and, ah!
The low, the deep, the pleading tone,
With which I sang another's Love,

Interpreted my own.

She listen'd with a flitting Blush,
With downcast Eyes and modest Grace;
And she forgave me, that I gaz'd
  Too fondly on her Face!

But when I told the cruel scorn
Which craz'd this bold and lovely Knight,
And that be cross'd the mountain woods
Nor rested day nor night;

That sometimes from the savage Den,
And sometimes from the darksome Shade,
And sometimes starting up at once
  In green and sunny Glade,

There came, and look'd him in the face,
An Angel beautiful and bright;
And that he knew, it was a Fiend,
  This miserable Knight!

And that, unknowing what he did,
He leapt amid a murd'rous Band,
And sav'd from Outrage worse than Death
  The Lady of the Land;

And how she wept and clasp'd his knees
And how she tended him in vain—
And ever strove to expiate
  The Scorn, that craz'd his Brain

And that she nurs'd him in a Cave;
And how his Madness went away
When on the yellow forest leaves
  A dying Man he lay;

His dying words—but when I reach'd
That tenderest strain of all the Ditty,
My falt'ring Voice and pausing Harp
Disturb'd her Soul with Pity!

All Impulses of Soul and Sense
Had thrill'd my guileless Genevieve,
The Music, and the doleful Tale, The
rich and balmy Eve;

And Hopes, and Fears that kindle Hope,
An undistinguishable Throng!
And gentle Wishes long subdued,
  Subdued and cherish'd long!

  She wept with pity and delight,
She blush'd with love and maiden shame;
And, like the murmur of a dream,
  I heard her breathe my name.

  Her Bosom heav'd—she stepp'd aside;
As conscious of my Look, she stepp'd—
Then suddenly with timorous eye
  She fled to me and wept.

  She half inclosed me with her arms,
She press'd me with a meek embrace;
And bending back her head look'd up,
  And gaz'd upon my face.

  'Twas partly Love, and partly Fear,
And partly 'twas a bashful Art
That I might rather feel than see
  The Swelling of her Heart.

  I calm'd her Tears; and she was calm,
And told her love with virgin Pride.
And so I won my Genevieve,
  My bright and beauteous Bride!

The MAD MOTHER.

  Her eyes are wild, her head is bare,
The sun has burnt her coal-black hair,
Her eye-brows have a rusty stain,
And she came far from over the main.
She has a baby on her arm,
Or else she were alone;
And underneath the hay-stack warm,
And on the green-wood stone,
She talked and sung the woods among;
And it was in the English tongue.

  "Sweet babe! they say that I am mad,
But nay, my heart is far too glad;
And I am happy when I sing

Full many a sad and doleful thing:
Then, lovely baby, do not fear!
I pray thee have no fear of me,
But, safe as in a cradle, here
My lovely baby! thou shalt be,
To thee I know too much I owe;
I cannot work thee any woe."

A fire was once within my brain;
And in my head a dull, dull pain; And
fiendish faces one, two, three, Hung
at my breasts, and pulled at me. But
then there came a sight of joy;
It came at once to do me good;
I waked, and saw my little boy,
My little boy of flesh and blood;
Oh joy for me that sight to see!
For he was here, and only he.

Suck, little babe, oh suck again!
It cools my blood; it cools my brain;
Thy lips I feel them, baby! they
Draw from my heart the pain away.
Oh! press me with thy little hand;
It loosens something at my chest;
About that tight and deadly band
I feel thy little fingers press'd.
The breeze I see is in the tree;
It comes to cool my babe and me.

Oh! love me, love me, little boy!
Thou art thy mother's only joy;
And do not dread the waves below,
When o'er the sea-rock's edge we go;
The high crag cannot work me harm,
Nor leaping torrents when they howl;
The babe I carry on my arm,
He saves for me my precious soul;
Then happy lie, for blest am I;
Without me my sweet babe would die.

Then do not fear, my boy! for thee
Bold as a lion I will be;
And I will always be thy guide,

Through hollow snows and rivers wide.
I'll build an Indian bower; I know
The leaves that make the softest bed:
And if from me thou wilt not go.
But still be true 'till I am dead,
My pretty thing! then thou shalt sing,
As merry as the birds in spring.

Thy father cares not for my breast,
'Tis thine, sweet baby, there to rest:
'Tis all thine own! and if its hue
Be changed, that was so fair to view,
'Tis fair enough for thee, my dove!
My beauty, little child, is flown;
But thou will live with me in love,
And what if my poor cheek be brown?
'Tis well for me, thou canst not see
How pale and wan it else would be.

Dread not their taunts, my little life!
I am thy father's wedded wife;
And underneath the spreading tree
We two will live in honesty.
If his sweet boy he could forsake,
With me he never would have stay'd:
From him no harm my babe can take,
But he, poor man! is wretched made,
And every day we two will pray
For him that's gone and far away.

I'll teach my boy the sweetest things;
I'll teach him how the owlet sings.
My little babe! thy lips are still,
And thou hast almost suck'd thy fill.
—Where art thou gone my own dear child?
What wicked looks are those I see?
Alas! alas! that look so wild,
It never, never came from me:
If thou art mad, my pretty lad,
Then I must be for ever sad.

Oh! smile on me, my little lamb!
For I thy own dear mother am.
My love for thee has well been tried:

I've sought thy father far and wide.
I know the poisons of the shade,
I know the earth-nuts fit for food;
Then, pretty dear, be not afraid;
We'll find thy father in the wood.
Now laugh and be gay, to the woods away!
And there, my babe; we'll live for aye.

THE ANCIENT MARINER,

A POET'S REVERIE.

ARGUMENT.

How a Ship, having first sailed to the Equator, was driven by Storms, to the cold Country towards the South Pole; how the Ancient Mariner cruelly, and in contempt of the laws of hospitality, killed a Sea-bird; and how he was followed by many and strange Judgements; and in what manner he came back to his own Country.

The ANCIENT MARINER.

A POET'S REVERIE.

I.

It is an ancient Mariner,
  And he stoppeth one of three:
"By thy long grey beard and thy glittering eye
  Now wherefore stoppest me?"

"The Bridegroom's doors are open'd wide
  And I am next of kin;
The Guests are met, the Feast is set,—
  May'st hear the merry din."

But still he holds the wedding guest—
  "There was a Ship, quoth he—"
"Nay, if thou'st got a laughsome tale,
  Mariner! come with me."

He holds him with his skinny hand,
  Quoth he, there was a Ship—
"Now get thee hence, thou grey-beard Loon
  Or my Staff shall make thee skip."

He holds him with his glittering eye—
  The wedding guest stood still
And listens like a three year's child;
  The Mariner hath his will.

The wedding-guest sate on a stone,
  He cannot chuse but hear:
And thus spake on that ancient man,
  The bright-eyed Mariner.

The Ship was cheer'd, the Harbour clear'd—
  Merrily did we drop
Below the Kirk, below the Hill,
  Below the Light-house top.

The Sun came up upon the left,
  Out of the Sea came he:
And he shone bright, and on the right
  Went down into the Sea.

Higher and higher every day,
  Till over the mast at noon—
The wedding-guest here beat his breast,
  For he heard the loud bassoon.

The Bride hath pac'd into the Hall,
  Red as a rose is she;
Nodding their heads before her goes
  The merry Minstralsy.

The wedding-guest he beat his breast,
  Yet he cannot chuse but hear:
And thus spake on that ancient Man,
  The bright-eyed Mariner.

But now the Northwind came more fierce,
  There came a Tempest strong!
And Southward still for days and weeks
  Like Chaff we drove along.

And now there came both Mist and Snow,
  And it grew wond'rous cold;
And Ice mast-high came floating by
  As green as Emerald.

And thro' the drifts the snowy clifts
  Did send a dismal sheen;
Nor shapes of men nor beasts we ken—
  The Ice was all between.

The Ice was here, the Ice was there,
  The Ice was all around:

It crack'd and growl'd, and roar'd and howl'd—
  A wild and ceaseless sound.

At length did cross an Albatross,
  Thorough the Fog it came;
As if it had been a Christian Soul,
  We hail'd it in God's name.

The Mariners gave it biscuit-worms,
  And round and round it flew:
The Ice did split with a Thunder-fit;
  The Helmsman steer'd us thro'.

And a good south wind sprung up behind.
  The Albatross did follow;
And every day for food or play
  Came to the Mariner's hollo!

In mist or cloud on mast or shroud
  It perch'd for vespers nine,
Whiles all the night thro' fog-smoke white
  Glimmer'd the white moon-shine.

"God save thee, ancient Mariner!
  From the fiends that plague thee thus—"
"Why look'st thou so?—with my cross bow
I shot the Albatross."

II:

The Sun now rose upon the right,
  Out of the Sea came he;
Still hid in mist; and on the left
  Went down into the Sea.

And the good south wind still blew behind,
  But no sweet Bird did follow
Nor any day for food or play
  Came to the Mariner's hollo!

And I had done an hellish thing
  And it would work e'm woe:
For all averr'd, I had kill'd the Bird
  That made the Breeze to blow.

Nor dim nor red, like an Angel's head,
  The glorious Sun uprist:
Then all averr'd, I had kill'd the Bird
  That brought the fog and mist.

'Twas right, said they, such birds to slay
  That bring the fog and mist.

The breezes blew, the white foam flew,
  The furrow follow'd free:
We were the first that ever burst
  Into that silent Sea.

Down dropt the breeze, the Sails dropt down,
  'Twas sad as sad could be
And we did speak only to break
  The silence of the Sea.

All in a hot and copper sky
  The bloody sun at noon,
Right up above the mast did stand,
  No bigger than the moon.

Day after day, day after day,
  We stuck, nor breath nor motion,
As idle as a painted Ship
  Upon a painted Ocean.

Water, water, every where
And all the boards did shrink;
Water, water, every where,
  Nor any drop to drink.

The very deeps did rot: O Christ!
  That ever this should be!
Yea, slimy things did crawl with legs
  Upon the slimy Sea.

About, about, in reel and rout
The Death-fires danc'd at night;
The water, like a witch's oils.
  Burnt green and blue and white.

And some in dreams assured were
Of the Spirit that plagued us so:
Nine fathom deep he had follow'd us
From the Land of Mist and Snow.

And every tongue thro' utter drouth
  Was wither'd at the root;
We could not speak no more than if
  We had been choked with soot.

Ah wel-a-day! what evil looks
  Had I from old and young;
Instead of the Cross the Albatross
  About my neck was hung.

III.

So past a weary time; each throat
  Was parch'd, and glaz'd each eye,
When, looking westward, I beheld
  A something in the sky.

At first it seem'd a little speck
  And then it seem'd a mist:
It mov'd and mov'd, and took at last
  A certain shape, I wist.

A speck, a mist, a shape, I wist!
  And still it near'd and near'd;
And, as if it dodg'd a water-sprite,
  It plung'd and tack'd and veer'd.

With throat unslack'd, with black lips bak'd
  We could nor laugh nor wail;
Thro' utter drouth all dumb we stood
Till I bit my arm and suck'd the blood,
  And cry'd, A sail! a sail!

With throat unslack'd, with black lips bak'd
  Agape they heard me call:
Gramercy! they for joy did grin
And all at once their breath drew in
  As they were drinking all.

See! See! (I cry'd) she tacks no more!
  Hither to work us weal
Without a breeze, without a tide
  She steddies with upright keel!

The western wave was all a flame,

The day was well nigh done!
Almost upon the western wave
  Rested the broad bright Sun;
When that strange shape drove suddenly
  Betwixt us and the Sun.

And strait the Sun was fleck'd with bars
  (Heaven's mother send us grace)
As if thro' a dungeon grate he peer'd
  With broad and burning face.

Alas! (thought I, and my heart beat loud)
  How fast she nears and nears!
Are those *her* Sails that glance in the Sun
  Like restless gossameres?

Are those *her* Ribs, thro' which the Sun
  Did peer, as thro' a grate?
And are those two all, all her crew.
  That Woman, and her Mate?

His bones were black with many a crack,
  All black and bare, I ween;
Jet-black and bare, save where with rust
Of mouldy damps and charnel crust
  They were patch'd with purple and green.

Her lips were red, *her* looks were free,
  Her locks were yellow as gold:
Her skin was as white as leprosy,
And she was far liker Death than he;
  Her flesh made the still air cold.

The naked Hulk alongside came
  And the Twain were playing dice;
"The Game is done! I've won, I've won!"
  Quoth she, and whistled thrice.

A gust of wind sterte up behind
  And whistled thro' his bones;
Thro' the holes of his eyes and the hole of his mouth
  Half-whistles and half-groans.

With never a whisper in the Sea
  Off darts the Spectre-ship;
While clombe above the Eastern bar

The horned Moon, with one bright Star
  Almost between the tips.

One after one by the horned Moon
  (Listen, O Stranger! to me)
Each turn'd his face with a ghastly pang
  And curs'd me with his ee.

Four times fifty living men,
  With never a sigh or groan,
With heavy thump, a lifeless lump
  They dropp'd down one by one.

Their souls did from their bodies fly,—
  They fled to bliss or woe;
And every soul it pass'd me by,
  Like, the whiz of my Cross-bow.

IV.

"I fear thee, ancient Mariner!
  I fear thy skinny hand;
And thou art long and lank and brown
  As is the ribb'd Sea-sand."

"I fear thee and thy glittering eye
  And thy skinny hand so brown—"
"Fear not, fear not, thou wedding guest!
  This body dropt not down."

Alone, alone, all all alone
Alone on the wide wide Sea;
And Christ would take no pity on
My soul in agony.

The many men so beautiful,
  And they all dead did lie!
And a million million slimy things
  Liv'd on—and so did I.

I look'd upon the rotting Sea,
  And drew my eyes away;
I look'd upon the ghastly deck,
  And there the dead men lay.

I look'd to Heaven, and try'd to pray;
  But or ever a prayer had gusht,
A wicked whisper came and made
  My heart as dry as dust.

I clos'd my lids and kept them close,
  Till the balls like pulses beat;
For the sky and the sea, and the sea and the sky
Lay like a load on my weary eye,
  And the dead were at my feet.

The cold sweat melted from their limbs,
  Nor rot, nor reek did they;
The look with which they look'd on me,
  Had never pass'd away.

An orphan's curse would drag to Hell
  A spirit from on high:
But O! more horrible than that
  Is the curse in a dead man's eye!
Seven days, seven nights I saw that curse,
  And yet I could not die.

The moving Moon went up the sky
  And no where did abide:
Softly she was going up
  And a star or two beside—

Her beams bemock'd the sultry main
  Like April hoar-frost spread;
But where the ship's huge shadow lay,
The charmed water burnt alway
  A still and awful red.

Beyond the shadow of the ship
  I watch'd the water-snakes:
They mov'd in tracks of shining white;
And when they rear'd, the elfish light
Fell off in hoary flakes.

Within the shadow of the ship
  I watch'd their rich attire:
Blue, glossy green, and velvet black
They coil'd and swam; and every track
Was a flash of golden fire.

O happy living things! no tongue
  Their beauty might declare:
A spring of love gusht from my heart,
  And I bless'd them unaware!
Sure my kind saint took pity on me,
  And I bless'd them unaware.

  The self-same moment I could pray;
  And from my neck so free
The Albatross fell off, and sank
  Like lead into the sea.

V.

  O sleep, it is a gentle thing
  Belov'd from pole to pole!
To Mary-queen the praise be given
She sent the gentle sleep from heaven
That slid into my soul.

  The silly buckets on the deck
  That had so long remain'd,
I dreamt that they were fill'd with dew
  And when I awoke it rain'd.

  My lips were wet, my throat was cold,
  My garments all were dank;
Sure I had drunken in my dreams
  And still my body drank.

  I mov'd and could not feel my limbs,
  I was so light, almost
I thought that I had died in sleep,
  And was a blessed Ghost.

  And soon I heard a roaring wind,
  It did not come anear;
But with its sound it shook the sails
  That were so thin and sere.

  The upper air burst into life
  And a hundred fire-flags sheen
To and fro they were hurried about;
And to and fro, and in and out

The wan stars danc'd between.

And the coming wind did roar more loud;
And the sails did sigh like sedge:
And the rain pour'd down from one black cloud
The moon was at its edge.

The thick black cloud was cleft, and still
The Moon was at its side:
Like waters shot from some high crag,
The lightning fell, with never a jag
A river steep and wide.

The loud wind never reach'd the Ship,
Yet now the Ship mov'd on!
Beneath the lightning and the moon
The dead men gave a groan.

They groan'd; they stirr'd, they all uprose,
Nor spake, nor mov'd their eyes:
It had been strange, even in a dream
To have seen those dead men rise,

The helmsman steerd, the ship mov'd on;
Yet never a breeze up-blew;
The Mariners all gan work the ropes,
Where they were wont to do:
They rais'd their limbs like lifeless tools—
We were a ghastly crew.

The body of my brother's son
Stood by me knee to knee:
The body and I pull'd at one rope,
But he said nought to me.

"I fear thee, ancient Mariner!"
"Be calm, thou wedding guest!
'Twas not those souls, that fled in pain,
Which to their corses came again,
But a troop of Spirits blest:"

"For when it dawn'd—they dropp'd their arms,
And cluster'd round the mast:
Sweet sounds rose slowly thro' their mouths
And from their bodies pass'd."

Around, around, flew each sweet sound,

Then darted to the sun:
Slowly the sounds came back again
  Now mix'd, now one by one.

Sometimes a dropping from the sky
I heard the Sky-lark sing;
Sometimes all little birds that are
How they seem'd to fill the sea and air
  With their sweet jargoning.

And now 'twas like all instruments,
  Now like a lonely flute;
And now it is an angel's song
  That makes the heavens be mute.

It ceas'd: yet still the sails made on
  A pleasant noise till noon,
A noise like of a hidden brook
  In the leafy month of June,
That to the sleeping woods all night,
  Singeth a quiet tune.

Till noon we silently sail'd on
  Yet never a breeze did breathe:
Slowly and smoothly went the Ship
  Mov'd onward from beneath.

Under the keel nine fathom deep
From the land of mist and snow
The spirit slid: and it was He
That made the Ship to go.
The sails at noon left off their tune
  And the Ship stood still also.

The sun right up above the mast
  Had fix'd her to the ocean:
But in a minute she 'gan stir
  With a short uneasy motion—
Backwards and forwards half her length
  With a short uneasy motion.

Then, like a pawing horse let go,
  She made a sudden bound:
It flung the blood into my head,
  And I fell into a swound.

How long in that same fit I lay,
  I have not to declare;
But ere my living life return'd,
I heard and in my soul discern'd
  Two voices in the air.

"Is it he?" quoth one, "Is this the man?
  By him who died on cross,
With his cruel bow he lay'd full low
  The harmless Albatross."

"The spirit who 'bideth by himself
  In the land of mist and snow,
He lov'd the bird that lov'd the man
  Who shot him with his bow."

The other was a softer voice,
  As soft as honey-dew:
Quoth he the man hath penance done,
  And penance more will do.

VI.

FIRST VOICE.

"But tell me, tell me! speak again,
  Thy soft response renewing—
What makes that ship drive on so fast?
  What is the Ocean doing?"

SECOND VOICE.

"Still as a Slave before his Lord,
  The Ocean hath no blast:
His great bright eye most silently
  Up to the moon is cast—"

"If he may know which way to go,
  For she guides him smooth or grim,
See, brother, see! how graciously
  She looketh down on him."

FIRST VOICE.

"But why drives on that ship so fast
Without or wave or wind?"

SECOND VOICE.

"The air is cut away before,
And closes from behind."

"Fly, brother, fly! more high, more high,
Or we shall be belated:
For slow and slow that ship will go,
When the Mariner's trance is abated."

I woke, and we were sailing on
As in a gentle weather:
'Twas night, calm night, the moon was high;
The dead men stood together.

All stood together on the deck,
For a charnel-dungeon fitter:
All fix'd on me their stony eyes
That in the moon did glitter.

The pang, the curse, with which they died,
Had never pass'd away;
I could not draw my eyes from theirs
Nor turn them up to pray.

And now this spell was snapt: once more
I view'd the ocean green,
And look'd far forth, yet little saw
Of what had else been seen.

Like one, that on a lonesome road
Doth walk in fear and dread,
And having once turn'd round, walks on
And turns no more his head:
Because he knows, a frightful fiend
Doth close behind him tread.

But soon there breath'd a wind on me,
Nor sound nor motion made:
Its path was not upon the sea
In ripple or in shade.

It rais'd my hair, it fann'd my cheek,

Like a meadow-gale of spring—
It mingled strangely with my fears,
Yet it felt like a welcoming.

Swiftly, swiftly flew the ship
Yet she sail'd softly too:
Sweetly, sweetly blew the breeze—
On me alone it blew.

O dream of joy! is this indeed
The light-house top I see?
Is this the Hill? Is this the Kirk?
Is this mine own countrée?

We drifted o'er the Harbour-bar,
And I with sobs did pray—
"O let me be awake, my God!
Or let me sleep alway!"

The harbour-bay was clear as glass,
So smoothly it was strewn!
And on the bay the moonlight lay,
And the shadow of the moon.

The rock shone bright, the kirk no less:
That stands above the rock:
The moonlight steep'd in silentness
The steady weathercock.

And the bay was white with silent light,
Till rising from the same
Full many shapes, that shadows were,
In crimson colours came.

A little distance from the prow
Those crimson shadows were:
I turn'd my eyes upon the deck—
O Christ! what saw I there?

Each corse lay flat, lifeless and flat;
And by the Holy rood
A man all light, a seraph-man,
On every corse there stood.

This seraph-band, each wav'd his hand:
It was a heavenly sight:
They stood as signals to the land,

Each one a lovely light:

This seraph-band, each wav'd his hand,
  No voice did they impart—
No voice; but O! the silence sank,
  Like music on my heart.

But soon I heard the dash of oars,
  I heard the pilot's cheer:
My head was turn'd perforce away
  And I saw a boat appear.

The pilot, and the pilot's boy
  I heard them coming fast:
Dear Lord in Heaven! it was a joy,
  The dead men could not blast.

I saw a third—I heard his voice:
  It is the Hermit good!
He singeth loud his godly hymns
  That he makes in the wood.
He'll shrive my soul, he'll wash away
  The Albatross's blood.

VII.

This Hermit good lives in that wood
  Which slopes down to the Sea.
How loudly his sweet voice he rears!
He loves to talk with Mariners
  That come from a far countrée.

He kneels at morn and noon and eve—
  He hath a cushion plump:
It is the moss, that wholly hides
  The rotted old Oak-stump.

The Skiff-boat ner'd: I heard them talk,
  "Why, this is strange, I trow!
Where are those lights so many and fair
  That signal made but now?"

"Strange, by my faith!" the Hermit said—
  "And they answer'd not our cheer.
The planks look warp'd, and see those sails

How thin they are and sere!
I never saw aught like to them
Unless perchance it were"

"The skeletons of leaves that lag
   My forest brook along:
When the Ivy-tod is heavy with snow,
And the Owlet whoops to the wolf below
   That eats the she-wolf's young."

"Dear Lord! it has a fiendish look—"
   (The Pilot made reply)
"I am a-fear'd."—"Push on, push on!"
   "Said the Hermit cheerily."

The Boat came closer to the Ship,
   But I nor spake nor stirr'd!
The Boat came close beneath the Ship,
   And strait a sound was heard!

Under the water it rumbled on,
   Still louder and more dread:
It reach'd the Ship, it split the bay;
   The Ship went down like lead.

Stunn'd by that loud and dreadful sound,
   Which sky and ocean smote:
Like one that hath been seven days drown'd
   My body lay afloat:
But, swift as dreams, myself I found
   Within the Pilot's boat.

Upon the whirl, where sank the Ship,
   The boat spun round and round:
And all was still, save that the hill
   Was telling of the sound.

I mov'd my lips: the Pilot shriek'd
   And fell down in a fit.
The Holy Hermit rais'd his eyes
   And pray'd where he did sit.

I took the oars: the Pilot's boy,
   Who now doth crazy go,
Laugh'd loud and long, and all the while
   His eyes went to and fro,

"Ha! ha!" quoth he—"full plain I see,
  The devil knows how to row."

And now all in mine own Countrée
  I stood on the firm land!
The Hermit stepp'd forth from the boat,
  And scarcely he could stand.

"O shrieve me, shrieve me, holy Man!"
  The Hermit cross'd his brow—
"Say quick," quoth he, "I bid thee say
  What manner man art thou?"

Forthwith this frame of mind was wrench'd
  With a woeful agony,
Which forc'd me to begin my tale
  And then it left me free.

Since then at an uncertain hour,
  That agency returns;
And till my ghastly tale is told
  This heart within me burns.

I pass, like night, from land to land;
  I have strange power of speech;
The moment that his face I see
I know the man that must hear me;
  To him my tale I teach.

What loud uproar bursts from that door!
  The Wedding-guests are there;
But in the Garden-bower the Bride
  And Bride-maids singing are:
And hark the little Vesper-bell
  Which biddeth me to prayer.

O Wedding-guest! this soul hath been
  Alone on a wide wide sea:
So lonely 'twas, that God himself
  Scarce seemed there to be.

O sweeter than the Marriage-feast,
  'Tis sweeter far to me
To walk together to the Kirk
  With a goodly company.

To walk together to the Kirk

And all together pray,
While each to his great father bends,
Old men, and babes, and loving friends,
And Youths, and Maidens gay.

Farewell, farewell! but this I tell
To thee, thou wedding-guest!
He prayeth well who loveth well
Both man, and bird and beast.

He prayeth best who loveth best
All things both great and small:
For the dear God, who loveth us,
He made and loveth all.

The Mariner, whose eye is bright,
Whose beard with age is hoar,
Is gone; and now the wedding-guest
Turn'd from the bridegroom's door.

He went, like one that hath been stunn'd
And is of sense forlorn:
A sadder and a wiser man
He rose the morrow morn,

LINES
Written a few miles above TINTERN ABBEY, an revisiting the banks of
the WYE during a Tour.
July 13, 1798.

Five years have passed; five summers, with the length
Of five long winters! and again I hear
These waters, rolling from their mountain-springs
With a sweet inland murmur. [6]—Once again
Do I behold these steep and lofty cliffs,
Which on a wild secluded scene impress
Thoughts of more deep seclusion; and connect
The landscape with the quiet of the sky.

[Footnote 6: The river is not affacted by the tides a few miles above Tintern.]

The day is come when I again repose
Here, under this dark sycamore, and view
These plots of cottage-ground, these orchard-tufts,
Which, at this season, with their unripe fruits,
Among the woods and copses lose themselves,

Nor, with their green and simple hue, disturb
The wild green landscape. Once again I see
These hedge-rows, hardly hedge-rows, little lines
Of sportive wood run wild; these pastoral farms
Green to the very door; and wreathes of smoke
Sent up, in silence, from among the trees,
With some uncertain notice, as might seem,
Of vagrant dwellers in the houseless woods,
Or of some hermit's cave, where by his fire
The hermit sits alone.

   Though absent long.
These forms of beauty have not been to me,
As is a landscape to a blind man's eye:
But oft, in lonely rooms, and mid the din
Of towns and cities, I have owed to them,
In hours of wariness, sensations sweet,
Felt in the blood, and felt along the heart,
And passing even into my purer mind,

   With tranquil restoration:—feelings too
Of unremembered pleasure: such, perhaps,
As may have had no trivial influence
On that best portion of a good man's life;
His little, nameless, unremembered acts
Of kindness and of love. Nor less, I trust,
To them I may have owed another gift,
Of aspect more sublime; that blessed mood,
In which the burthen of the mystery,
In which the heavy and the weary weight
Of all this unintelligible world
Is lighten'd:—that serene and blessed mood;
In which the affections gently lead us on,
Until, the breath of this corporeal frame,
And even the motion of our human blood
Almost suspended, we are laid asleep
In body, and become a living soul:
While with an eye made quiet by the power
Of harmony, and the deep power of joy,
We see into the life of things.

  If this
Be but a vain belief, yet, oh! how oft,

In darkness, and amid the many shapes
Of joyless day-light; when the fretful stir
Unprofitable, and the fever of the world,
Have hung upon the beatings of my heart,
How oft, in spirit, have I turned to thee
O sylvan Wye! Thou wanderer through the woods,
How often has my spirit turned to thee!

  And now, with gleams, of half-extinguish'd thought,
With many recognitions dim and faint,
And somewhat of a sad perplexity,
The picture of the mind revives again:
While here I stand, not only with the sense
Of present pleasure, but with pleasing thoughts
That in this moment there is life and food
For future years. And so I dare to hope
Though changed, no doubt, from what I was, when first
I came among these hills; when like a roe
I bounded o'er the mountains, by the sides
Of the deep rivers, and the lonely streams,
Wherever nature led: more like a man
Flying from something that he dreads, than one
Who sought the thing he loved. For nature then
(The coarser pleasures of my boyish days,
And their glad animal movements all gone by,)
To me was all in all.—I cannot paint
What then I was. The sounding cataract
Haunted me like a passion: the tall rock,
The mountain, and the deep and gloomy wood,
Their colours and their forms, were then to me
An appetite: a feeling and a love,
That had no need of a remoter charm,
By thought supplied, or any interest
Unborrowed from the eye.—That time is past,
And all its aching joys are now no more,
And all its dizzy raptures. Not for this
Faint I, nor mourn nor murmur: other gifts
Have followed, for such loss, I would believe
Abundant recompence. For I have learned
To look on nature, not as in the hour
Of thoughtless youth, but hearing oftentimes
The still, sad music of humanity,

Nor harsh nor grating, though of ample power
To chasten and subdue. And I have felt
A presence that disturbs me with the joy
Of elevated thoughts; a sense sublime
Of something far more deeply interfused,
Whose dwelling is the light of setting suns,
And the round ocean, and the living air,
And the blue sky, and in the mind of man,
A motion and a spirit, that impels
All thinking things, all objects of all thought,
And rolls through all things. Therefore am I still
A lover of the meadows and the woods,
And mountains; and of all that we behold
From this green earth; of all the mighty world
Of eye and ear; both what they half create, [7]
And what perceive; well pleased to recognize
In nature and the language of the sense,
The anchor of my purest thoughts, the nurse,
The guide, the guardian of my heart, and soul
Of all my moral being.

[Footnote 7: This line has a close resemblance to an admirable line of Young, the exact expression of which I cannot recollect.]

          Nor, perchance,
If I were not thus taught, should I the more
Suffer my genial spirits to decay?
For thou art with me, here, upon the banks
Of this fair river; thou, my dearest Friend,
My dear, dear Friend, and in thy voice I catch
The language of my former heart, and read
My former pleasures in the shooting lights
Of thy wild eyes. Oh! yet a little while
May I behold in thee what I was once,
My dear, dear Sister! And this prayer I make,
Knowing that Nature never did betray
The heart that loved her; 'tis her privilege,
Through all the years of this our life, to lead
From joy to joy: for she can so inform
The mind that is within us, so impress
With quietness and beauty, and so feed
With lofty thoughts, that neither evil tongues,
Rash judgments, nor the sneers of selfish men,

Nor greetings where no kindness is, nor all
The dreary intercourse of daily life,
Shall e'er prevail against us, or disturb
Our chearful faith that all which we behold
Is full of blessings. Therefore let the moon
Shine on thee in thy solitary walk;
And let the misty mountain winds be free
To blow against thee: and in after years,
When these wild ecstasies shall be matured
Into a sober pleasure, when thy mind
Shall be a mansion for all lovely forms,
Thy memory be as a dwelling-place
For all sweet sounds and harmonies; Oh! then,
If solitude, or fear, or pain, or grief,
Should be thy portion, with what healing thoughts
Of tender joy wilt thou remember me,
And these my exhortations! Nor perchance,
If I should be, where I no more can hear
Thy voice, nor catch from thy wild eyes these gleams
Of past existence, wilt thou then forget
That on the banks of this delightful stream
We stood together; and that I, so long
A worshipper of Nature, hither came,
Unwearied in that service: rather say
With warmer love, oh! with far deeper zeal
Of holier love. Nor wilt thou then forget,
That after many wanderings, many years
Of absence, these steep woods and lofty cliffs,
And this green pastoral landscape, were to me
More dear, both for themselves, and for thy sake.

NOTES

NOTE to THE THORN—This Poem ought to have been preceded by an introductory Poem, which I have been prevented from writing by never having felt myself in a mood when it was probable that I should write it well. —The character which I have here introduced speaking is sufficiently common. The Reader will perhaps have a general notion of it, if he has ever known a man, a Captain of a small trading vessel for example, who being past the middle age of life, had retired upon an annuity or small independent income to some village or country town of which he was not a native, or in which he had not been accustomed to live. Such men having little to do become credulous and talkative from indolence; and from the same cause, and other predisposing causes by which it is probable that such men may have been affected, they are prone to superstition. On which account it appeared to me proper to select a character like this to exhibit some of the general laws by which superstition acts upon the mind. Superstitious men are almost always men of slow faculties and deep feelings; their minds are not loose but adhesive; they have a reasonable share of imagination, by which word I mean the faculty which produces impressive effects out of simple elements; but they are utterly destitute of fancy, the power by which pleasure and surprize are excited by sudden varieties of situation and by accumulated imagery.

It was my wish in this poem to shew the manner in which such men cleave to the same ideas; and to follow the turns of passion, always different, yet not palpably different, by which their conversation is swayed. I had two objects to attain; first, to represent a picture which should not be unimpressive yet consistent with the character that should describe it, secondly, while I adhered to the style in which such persons describe, to take care that words, which in their minds are impregnated with passion, should likewise convey passion to Readers who are not accustomed to sympathize with men feeling in that manner or using such language. It seemed to me that this might be done by calling in the assistance of Lyrical and rapid Metre. It was necessary that the Poem, to be natural, should in reality move slowly; yet I hoped, that, by the aid of the metre, to those who should at all enter into the spirit of the Poem, it would appear to move quickly. The Reader will have the kindness to excuse this note as I am sensible that an introductory Poem is necessary to give this Poem its full effect.

Upon this occasion I will request permission to add a few words closely connected with THE THORN and many other Poems in these Volumes. There is a numerous class of readers who imagine that the same words cannot be repeated without tautology: this is a great error: virtual tautology is much oftener produced by using different words when the meaning is exactly the same. Words, a Poet's words more particularly, ought to be weighed in the balance of feeling and not measured by the space which they occupy upon paper. For the Reader cannot be too often reminded that Poetry is passion: it is the history or science of feelings: now every man must know that an attempt is rarely made to communicate impassioned feelings without something of an accompanying consciousness of the inadequateness of our own powers, or the deficiencies of language. During such efforts there will be a craving in the mind, and as long as it is unsatisfied the Speaker will cling to the same words, or words of the same character. There are also various other reasons why repetition and apparent tautology are frequently beauties of the highest kind. Among the chief of these reasons is the interest which the mind attaches to words, not only as symbols of the passion, but as *things*, active and efficient, which are of themselves part of the passion. And further, from a spirit of fondness, exultation, and gratitude, the mind luxuriates in the repetition of words which appear successfully to communicate its feelings. The truth of these remarks might be shewn by innumerable passages from the Bible and from the impassioned poetry of every nation.

"Awake, awake Deborah: awake, awake, utter a song:"

"Arise Barak, and lead thy captivity captive, thou Son of Abinoam."

"At her feet he bowed, he fell, he lay down: at her feet he bowed, he fell; where he bowed there he fell down dead."

"Why is his Chariot so long in coming? Why tarry the Wheels of his Chariot?"—Judges, Chap. 5th. Verses 12th, 27th, and part of 28th.
—See also the whole of that tumultuous and wonderful Poem.

NOTE to the ANCIENT MARINER, p. 155.—I cannot refuse myself the gratification of informing such Readers as may have been pleased with this Poem, or with any part of it, that they owe their pleasure in some sort to me; as the Author was himself very desirous that it should be suppressed. This wish had arisen from a consciousness of the defects of the Poem, and from a knowledge that many persons had been much displeased with it. The Poem of my Friend has indeed great defects; first, that the principal person has no distinct character, either in his profession of Mariner, or as a human being who having been long under the controul of supernatural impressions might be supposed himself to partake of something supernatural: secondly, that he does not act, but is continually acted upon: thirdly, that the events having no necessary connection do not produce each other; and lastly, that the imagery is somewhat too laboriously accumulated. Yet the Poem contains many delicate touches of passion, and indeed the passion is every where true to nature; a great number of the stanzas present beautiful images, and are expressed with unusual felicity of language; and the versification, though the metre is itself unfit for long poems, is harmonious and artfully varied, exhibiting the utmost powers of that metre, and every variety of which it is capable. It therefore appeared to me that these several merits (the first of which, namely that of the passion, is of the highest kind,) gave to the Poem a value which is not often possessed by better Poems. On this account I requested of my Friend to permit me to republish it.

NOTE to the Poem ON REVISITING THE WYE, p. 201.—I have not ventured to call this Poem an Ode; but it was written with a hope that in the transitions, and the impassioned music of the versification would be found the principal requisites of that species of composition.

END OF VOL. I.

Ingram Content Group UK Ltd.
Milton Keynes UK
UKHW011944270323
419267UK00003B/46